12 Days

of

Eldritch Yule

'Twas the Abyss Before Yuletide

In the unfathomable eve before Yule, when all within the eldritch dwelling lay ensnared in a preternatural trance,

Not a single entity stirred, not even the most minuscule aberration dared to dance;

The stockings, suspended with an eldritch precision, clung to the ethereal hearth with malevolent care,

In hopes that the cosmic harbinger, veiled in eldritch shroud, would soon materialize there;

The children, cradled in the eldritch embrace of their spectral beds,

Witnessed visions of nightmarish realms and eldritch sugar-plums cavorting in their fevered heads;

And the maternal figure, enshrouded in a spectral cloak, and the author in his occult cap,

Had just fortified their minds for a protracted sojourn in the realm of eldritch nap,

When upon the spectral grounds there manifested an otherworldly cacophony,

I sprang from the bed to witness the intrusion of what blasphemous anomaly.

Away to the window, I hastened like a fleeting apparition,

Tore open the shutters, revealing a portal to an alien dimension.

The moon, casting its eldritch glow upon the newly fallen cosmic snow,

Bestowed an eerie luminescence upon the eldritch tableau below.

Before my bewildered eyes transpired an aberration of cosmic dread,

A miniature sleigh and eight abominable coursers, guided by a spectral driver, so lively and dread,

I knew in that moment, it was the harbinger of cosmic horror, St. Nick.

More rapid than eldritch tempests, his coursers they came,

And he whistled, and shouted, and called them by eldritch name;

"Now, Dasher! now, Dancer! now, Prancer and Vixen!

On, Comet! on, Cupid! on, Donder and Blitzen!

To the zenith of the spectral porch! to the apices of the spectral wall!

Now dash away! dash away! dash away all!"

Like spectral leaves before an otherworldly maelstrom take flight,

They ascended to the house-top, vanishing into the eldritch night;

With a sleigh filled with forbidden artifacts, and St. Nicholas astride,

A spectral figure emerged as the eldritch sleigh did glide.

In a cosmic twinkling, I heard upon the ethereal rooftop,

The prancing and pawing of each spectral hoof's malevolent clop.

As I withdrew my head, turning with a spectral twist,

Down the cosmic chimney St. Nicholas descended with an eldritch tryst.

Cloaked in otherworldly fur from head to foot,

His attire adorned with the malevolence of interdimensional soot;

A bundle of forbidden cosmic artifacts slung upon his back,

He resembled a peddler of eldritch wares, his spectral pack unpacked.

His eyes—how they gleamed with the madness of cosmic mirth!

His spectral cheeks like nebulous roses, his nose a celestial cherry's unearthly girth!

His droll mouth drawn in an eldritch bow,

And the beard of his chin as white as cosmic snow;

A stump of a pipe clenched in his teeth with spectral grace,

Its smoke forming eldritch halos in the astral space;

A broad face and a little round belly,

That shook with eldritch laughter, like a bowlful of cosmic jelly.

He was plump and spectral, a jolly eldritch sprite,

And I laughed in the face of cosmic awe, in spite of the eldritch fright;

A wink of his eye and a twist of his head,

Assured me of eldritch tranquility, filling my heart with spectral stead.

He spoke not a word, but commenced his eldritch chore,

Filling each stocking with eldritch gifts galore;

Then with an eldritch nod and a touch of his nose,

Up the cosmic chimney, in eldritch repose;

He sprung to his sleigh, to his team gave an eldritch whistle,

And away they all vanished like the eldritch down of a cosmic thistle;

But I heard him exclaim, as he transcended beyond eldritch sight,

"Unearthly Yuletide to all, and to all an eldritch night."

Foreword

In the dim recesses of the cosmic unknown, where shadows dance with eldritch whispers, I extend a cryptic invitation to the intrepid souls who dare to tread upon the threshold of the extraordinary. Here, within the pages of "12 Nights of Eldritch Yule," a tapestry of cosmic horror unfolds, interwoven with the enduring traditions of Christmas. The air is pregnant with a peculiar tension. This subtle disquiet heralds the convergence of the eerie and the festive.

Picture the hallowed halls of the astral library, where the Canticles of Yule lay dormant, awaiting discovery. As the veil between worlds thins, I set the stage, beckoning readers to traverse realms where Eldritch Entities and the Yuletide spirit collide in a macabre waltz.

What follows is a journey through the twelve nights, each tale an offering to the eldritch forces that lurk in the shadows, eager to partake in the merriment of Christmas. Let the atmosphere seep into your senses, casting a spell transcending mere fiction's boundaries. Here, you are not a passive observer but an accomplice to the cosmic dance, a witness to the union of terror and festivity.

The inspiration behind these tales is a symphony of the bizarre and the familiar, conducted by me—a maestro of cosmic unease. The echoes of eldritch horrors reverberate alongside the twinkling lights of Christmas, creating a harmony that resonates in the deepest corners of the imagination.

As you turn the pages, know that you traverse the winding narratives of each tale and the labyrinthine corridors of my vision. The darkness is not a foe but a companion, guiding you through realms where the ordinary and the cosmic entwine in an embrace that defies the conventional.

Dear reader, embark now on this odyssey of unsettling beauty. I extend a hand, inviting you to partake in the enigma "12 Nights of Eldritch Yule." May the shadows cast by festive lights be the heralds of a cosmic revelation, and may the echoes of eldritch whispers linger in the recesses of your consciousness long after the final night has passed.

In the delicate dance between light and shadow, where the yuletide glow intertwines with the stygian mysteries, I extend a personal invitation to journey through the realms of "12 Nights of Eldritch Yule." This foreword serves as a lantern, casting its glow upon the intentions that dance within the pages, illuminating the path where tradition and terror converge.

Within the spectral pages of this anthology, the intention is clear—to weave the tapestry of traditional Christmas tales with the spine-chilling allure of Lovecraftian cosmic horror. This literary experiment is not merely an amalgamation of genres but an invocation—an attempt to summon the eldritch forces that slumber within the folds of festive traditions.

Picture the crackling fireplace adorned with stockings hung in anticipation, yet know that those very stockings may become portals to celestial realms within these tales. The intention is not to dismantle the cherished traditions of Christmas but to drape them in a cosmic veil, revealing hidden dimensions where the unknown commingles with the familiar.

In the fusion of cosmic horror and Christmas, I aspire to evoke a sense of wonder and disquiet, blurring the boundaries between the ordinary and the extraordinary. The intention is not to terrify for the sake of fear alone but to illuminate the shadows that linger beneath the tinsel and the ornaments, inviting readers to confront the cosmic mysteries that dwell in the heart of the festive season.

As you embark on this journey, dear reader, let the intentions laid bare within these words guide your steps. Embrace the eldritch visions with an open mind, for within the cosmic embrace of the unknown, the true spirit of Christmas may find new expression. "12 Nights of Eldritch Yule" is more than a collection of tales—it is a cosmic celebration where the terrors of the void and the joys of the season entwine like ivy upon the pillars of tradition.

May this literary venture be a source of both disquiet and delight, a testament to the endless possibilities that arise when the mundane collides with the cosmic. I extend a hand, beckoning you to traverse the boundary between the festive and the eldritch, where the glow of Christmas illuminates the shadows, and the shadows, in turn, cast their eternal gaze upon the Yule.

In the ethereal tapestry woven by the cosmic loom, I unravel the threads that bind the mundane to the eldritch in the enigmatic pages of "12 Nights of Eldritch Yule." As the shadows lengthen and the festive lights flicker, there is a revelation to be shared—an unveiling of the muses that whispered secrets and inspirations throughout the creation of this otherworldly anthology.

From the very inception, the ink that flowed upon these pages was stirred by a blend of timeless allure and cosmic wonders. I peer into the depths of inspiration, where the muses revealed themselves in the guise of Christmas traditions and the eldritch echoes of Lovecraft's cosmic horror.

Imagine the timeless allure of Christmas traditions—the warmth of hearth and home, the joyous melodies that echo through snowy streets, and the wonder that dances in the eyes of those captivated by the season's magic. Within these moments, where nostalgia and tradition converge, the first muse revealed itself—a beacon illuminating the path toward tales that resonate with the spirit of Christmas.

Yet, equally potent were the echoes of cosmic wonders found within the works of Lovecraft. The eldritch horrors that sprawl across his tales, the astral entities that defy mortal comprehension, and the unfathomable mysteries that lurk beyond the veil of reality—they became the second muse. A muse that whispered of a cosmic dance where Christmas and horror entwine, birthing alchemy that transcends genres and beckons readers into uncharted realms.

As you delve into these pages, dear reader, know that the muses have left their indelible mark upon the ink, guiding the hand that penned the tales. The revelation of the muse is an acknowledgment that inspiration is a cosmic force drawn from the rich tapestry of tradition and the celestial wonders that have fueled the imagination across centuries.

So, embark on this odyssey with the understanding that the muses, both traditional and eldritch, have conspired to bring forth a collection where Christmas and cosmic horror converge, creating a literary kaleidoscope that refracts the beauty of tradition through the prism of the unknown. I invite you to traverse these realms, guided by the whispers of muses that echo through the corridors of tradition and cosmic wonders alike.

Amidst the realms where darkness and luminescence coalesce, I unveil yet another layer of intrigue within the foreword of "12 Nights of Eldritch Yule." In a dance of shadows and revelations, this segment promises to be more than a mere prologue—a cryptic invitation, a whispered promise of the enigmatic odyssey ahead.

I weave a tapestry of enigma as the quill dances upon the parchment. A masterful stroke of narrative magic unfolds as cryptic hints and teasers are scattered across these pages, each word a fragment of the cosmic puzzle waiting to be assembled.

Dear reader, within the ink-stained recesses of this foreword, you shall find whispers that echo through the corridors of time and space. Like riddles in the wind, these veiled clues invite you to unravel the mysteries that permeate the twelve nights of Yule. It is a challenge that transcends the boundaries of conventional storytelling, beckoning you to actively participate in the unraveling cosmic drama.

Keep a keen eye for the subtle tremors within the narrative—a fleeting shadow, a whispered name, or a slight change in the atmospheric currents as you read. These are not mere coincidences but deliberate breadcrumbs guiding you through the labyrinth of eldritch tales that await. The cryptic hints, like elusive constellations in a cosmic night sky, are there for those who seek to decode the celestial language I penned, Magnum Tenebrosum.

And so, with each turn of the page, let your imagination be the compass that navigates the veiled landscape of these cryptic hints and teasers. As you delve deeper into the foreboding unknown, remember that the revelations are not confined to the explicit; they are woven into the very fabric of the narrative, waiting for the astute reader to uncover the cosmic truths beneath the surface.

Prepare, dear reader, for the cryptic hints are the first whispers of the eldritch symphony that unfolds across the twelve nights of Yule. May your senses be heightened, your curiosity kindled, and your mind attuned to the cosmic cadence that resonates within my cryptic offerings. The journey begins here, where hints are cast like constellations, forming a celestial map that leads to the heart of the cosmic enigma.

In the interplay of shadows and revelation, I extend an ethereal hand, beckoning readers to traverse the foreword of "12 Nights of Eldritch Yule," where each word is a whispered covenant with the unknown. As the narrative unfolds, a spectral pact materializes—a bond forged between the reader and the cosmic horrors that await within the intricate tapestry of these pages.

As the spectral guide through these cosmic realms, I extend a covenant to all who dare to tread upon this eldritch odyssey. It is not merely an invitation but a pact with the unknown. This willingly forged alliance transcends the boundaries between the reader and the narrative.

,

As you immerse yourself in the following pages, reader, understand that you are not a passive observer but an active participant in the cosmic dance. I invite you to willingly surrender to the eldritch mysteries concealed within these tales. It is a covenant—a pact that binds your curiosity with the cosmic forces that slumber within the ink-stained tapestry.

As you surrender to the unknown, let the tendrils of imagination intertwine with the eldritch tendrils that creep across the narrative landscape. In the spirit of the pact, you become a co-conspirator with me, traversing the realms where the ordinary transforms into the extraordinary, where the festive is tinged with the cosmic, and where the unknown is unveiled through shared exploration.

Prepare to relinquish the familiar for the embrace of the arcane, for in this covenant, fear and wonder are but two sides of the same cosmic coin. I invite you to release your preconceptions and open yourself to the eldritch energies that resonate within the very fabric of these tales.

So, dear reader, heed the call of the cosmic covenant. Embrace the unknown with an open heart and a mind unshackled by the constraints of the commonplace. Your journey through the twelve nights of Yule is not a solitary venture; it is a shared covenant with me, where the unknown becomes a companion, and the eldritch becomes a muse in the symphony of your imagination. The pact is sealed, and the odyssey begins—a dance between the reader and the cosmic unknown that transcends the confines of conventional storytelling.

As the pen dances upon the parchment, I unfurl another layer of cosmic revelation within the foreword of "12 Nights of Eldritch Yule." The narrative subtly turns, gently reminding readers that once the journey commences, the veil between the ordinary and the cosmic will thin—an inescapable invitation to traverse realms where anticipation and dread become indistinguishable.

With each word inscribed, I delicately impart a subtle truth—a whispered caution that the journey embarked upon within these pages is one from which escape becomes an endeavor fraught with anticipation and dread. Once the cosmic threshold is crossed, the veil between the ordinary and the eldritch becomes a permeable membrane, inviting readers to traverse a realm where reality and cosmic fantasy intertwine.

As you embark on this inescapable journey through the twelve nights of Yule, recognize that the ordinary pathways will blur into the unknown. The landscapes painted are not mere illusions but gateways to dimensions where the festive cheer coexists with eldritch horrors. The invitation is clear—an entreaty to surrender to the cosmic forces that lie in wait within these tales.

Anticipation and dread become intertwined companions on this odyssey. The ordinary will yield to the extraordinary, and the familiar will be cloaked in the cosmic unknown. This inescapable invitation with the understanding that the reader willingly steps into the eldritch embrace, where the line between fear and fascination blurs into a dance of cosmic revelation.

As you turn the pages, let anticipation be your guide through the moonlit corridors and dread be the shadow that heightens the cosmic unease. There is no turning back once the journey commences, for the inescapable nature of the narrative ensures that the eldritch embrace becomes an indelible mark upon the reader's imagination.

Prepare, dear reader, for the veil between worlds will thin, and the escape from the eldritch embrace will be an endeavor woven with threads of anticipation and dread. The journey is inescapable, the cosmic dance inevitable, and within the pages of "12 Nights of Eldritch Yule," reality becomes a malleable tapestry shaped by the cosmic forces awaiting your arrival.

Magnum Tenebrosum

The Discovery of the Canticles

Prologue

In the heart of an ancient forgotten library, darkness clung to the pages of dusty tomes. Time had gnawed at the spines of once-revered books, and the air hung heavy with the scent of aged parchment. Flickering candlelight, the only source of illumination, cast dancing shadows on timeworn shelves, creating an otherworldly ballet of light and darkness.

Within this hallowed sanctuary of knowledge, Dr. Evelyn Blackthorn navigated the labyrinth of forgotten lore. Her footsteps echoed through the vaulted halls, a mere whisper against the vast tapestry of silence. The librarian's lantern swung gently from her grasp, its feeble glow revealing rows upon rows of books that seemed to stretch into eternity.

As Dr. Blackthorn ventured deeper, her discerning eyes caught the glint of something peculiar—an ornate tome nestled amidst the forgotten volumes. Its cover bore an intricate pattern, an arcane design that hinted at mysteries beyond mortal understanding. The Canticles of Yule lay dormant, waiting for the touch of a curious hand to awaken its eldritch secrets.

Unbeknownst to the world beyond the library's confines, a cosmic prophecy lay concealed within the Canticles. Professor Nathaniel Eldritch, a mysterious figure with knowledge that surpassed the boundaries of the known, stood in the shadowy recesses, observing the unfolding discovery. Once thought lost to time, the ancient tome held the key to a cosmic revelation that would intertwine the fates of those who celebrated Christmas with the eldritch entities that lurked beyond the veil of reality.

And so, within the forgotten library, the stage was set. Dr. Evelyn Blackthorn stumbled upon the

Canticles of Yule, her discovery setting in motion a cosmic prophecy that would weave together the destinies of unsuspecting celebrants and the eldritch forces that hungered for a connection to the festivities of the Yuletide season. The echoes of her footsteps resonated through the silent corridors, foreshadowing the cosmic dance that awaited in the twelve nights to come.

In the dim-lit corners of the forgotten library, Dr. Evelyn Blackthorn, an intrepid historian fueled by insatiable curiosity, stood at the precipice of a discovery that would reshape her understanding of reality. Her eyes, gleaming with the passion for unearthing forgotten truths, fixated on the Canticles of Yule—a tome wrapped in mystery and adorned with symbols hinting at untold cosmic secrets.

The librarian, Professor Nathaniel Eldritch, a figure draped in an air of mystery, observed Dr.

Blackthorn's every move. Cloaked in the shadowy recesses, he possessed an uncanny knowledge of the Canticles—a guardian of arcane secrets whose presence hinted at a deeper connection to the cosmic revelations about to unfold.

As Dr. Blackthorn gently opened the ancient tome, the pages whispered tales of Yuletide celebrations intertwined with eldritch forces. Professor Eldritch, his gaze unwavering, knew that the discovery would set in motion a cosmic symphony, with each note played on the strings of destiny.

The librarian's lantern cast elongated shadows as Dr. Blackthorn delved into the pages, deciphering the arcane language that spoke of entities beyond mortal comprehension. The Canticles, a dormant witness to centuries of Christmas celebrations, now stirred with the anticipation of an impending cosmic revelation.

In that hallowed moment within the forgotten library, the fates of Dr. Evelyn Blackthorn and Professor Nathaniel Eldritch became threads woven into the fabric of an eldritch tapestry. The stage was set, and the Canticles whispered secrets that transcended the boundaries of time and space. This ancient prophecy would cast its cosmic shadow upon the twelve nights of Yule.

In academia, Dr. Evelyn Blackthorn had carved a niche for herself, her scholarly pursuits a testament to a relentless quest for hidden truths. From dusty archives to forgotten tombs, she had tread where others hesitated, driven by an insatiable hunger for knowledge that surpassed the boundaries of conventional scholarship.

Her reputation as a seeker of hidden truths extended far beyond the walls of the forgotten library. Dr. Blackthorn's academic pursuits were as much a journey into forbidden territories as they were an exploration of the known. The corridors of ancient civilizations echoed with the echoes of her footsteps, each discovery adding another layer to her enigmatic persona.

In pursuit of forgotten lore, she had deciphered cryptic inscriptions in the ruins of ancient civilizations, daring to unveil the obscured histories that lay beneath the layers of time. The occult and the arcane were not mere subjects of academic inquiry for Dr. Blackthorn; they were gateways to realms where the ordinary yielded to the extraordinary.

Her colleagues spoke in hushed tones about the artifacts she had unearthed, each whisper carrying the weight of respect and a hint of trepidation. Dr. Blackthorn's academic pursuits were not for the faint of heart. She was a scholar unafraid to delve into the forbidden, a trailblazer whose insatiable curiosity led her to the brink of mysteries that eluded the grasp of her more conventional peers.

As the pages of history turned, Dr. Evelyn Blackthorn's name became synonymous with the pursuit of hidden truths, and her reputation as a scholar who danced on the edge of the arcane only grew. It was this reputation that drew her to the forgotten library. In this place, the whispers of cosmic revelations awaited, eager to add another chapter to the storied legacy of Dr. Blackthorn's academic pursuits.

Dr. Evelyn Blackthorn's lantern cast a feeble glow in the dim-lit recesses of the forgotten library, revealing the hallowed shelves lined with dusty tomes. Her discerning eyes, ever watchful for the glint of forgotten knowledge, caught a peculiar gleam amidst the ancient volumes—a subtle invitation from the Canticles of Yule.

As she approached, the air grew heavy with the scent of aged parchment, and the creaking floorboards beneath her echoed with the weight of untold histories. The Canticles, a forgotten tome hidden among the dusty volumes, lay in wait, its cover adorned with cryptic symbols that seemed to shift and dance in the flickering candlelight.

Dr. Blackthorn's fingers traced the intricate patterns on the cover, her touch awakening the slumbering echoes of cosmic mysteries. Once thought lost to the annals of time, the ancient tome radiated an aura that transcended the ordinary. Its very existence whispered tales of Yuletide celebrations intertwined with eldritch forces. This revelation beckoned to the historian's insatiable curiosity.

With bated breath, Dr. Blackthorn gently opened the Canticles, its pages crackling with the weight of forgotten prophecies. The arcane language within told of cosmic entities that stirred in the shadows, waiting to be awakened by the festive cheer of Christmas celebrations. At that moment, amidst the forgotten tomes and the hushed corridors of the library, Dr. Evelyn Blackthorn stumbled upon a cosmic revelation. This discovery would set the intricate dance between the ordinary and the eldritch across the twelve nights of Yule.

In the annals of academia, Dr. Evelyn Blackthorn had etched a legacy as a relentless seeker of hidden truths. Her scholarly pursuits were not confined to the well-trodden paths of conventional research but delved into the forbidden territories that dared others to follow.

Dr. Blackthorn's academic journey read like a tale of audacity and insatiable curiosity, from the dusty archives of ancient civilizations to the cryptic inscriptions of long-forgotten tombs. Unearthing artifacts that whispered secrets of bygone eras, she ventured where others hesitated, driven by a passion that surpassed the boundaries of conventional scholarship.

Colleagues spoke in hushed tones of her exploits, the artifacts she had uncovered, and the mysteries she had unraveled. Dr. Blackthorn was not merely a scholar but a trailblazer, a woman unafraid to dance on the edge of the arcane and confront the obscured histories beneath the layers of time.

The occult and the arcane were not mere subjects of academic inquiry for her; they were gateways to realms where the ordinary yielded to the extraordinary. The corridors of ancient civilizations echoed with the echoes of her footsteps, each discovery adding another layer to her enigmatic persona.

Her reputation as a seeker of hidden truths extended far beyond the walls of lecture halls and libraries. It was a legacy forged in the crucible of forbidden knowledge. It was an academic journey that blurred the lines between conventional wisdom and the eldritch mysteries that beckoned from the shadows.

As the pages of history turned, Dr. Evelyn Blackthorn's name became synonymous with the pursuit of hidden truths, and her reputation as a scholar who dared to tread where others feared to linger only grew. This audacious spirit drew her to the forgotten library, where the Canticles of Yule awaited—a place where the echoes of the past and the cosmic revelations of the future converged in an intricate dance.

Dr. Evelyn Blackthorn's lantern cast a feeble glow in the dim-lit recesses of the forgotten library, revealing the hallowed shelves lined with dusty tomes.

Her discerning eyes, ever watchful for the glint of forgotten knowledge, caught a peculiar gleam amidst the ancient volumes—a subtle invitation from the Canticles of Yule.

As she approached, the air grew heavy with the scent of aged parchment, and the creaking floorboards beneath her echoed with the weight of untold histories. The Canticles, a forgotten tome hidden among the dusty volumes, lay in wait, its cover adorned with cryptic symbols that seemed to shift and dance in the flickering candlelight.

Dr. Blackthorn's fingers traced the intricate patterns on the cover, her touch awakening the slumbering echoes of cosmic mysteries. Once thought lost to the annals of time, the ancient tome radiated an aura that transcended the ordinary. Its very existence whispered tales of Yuletide celebrations intertwined with eldritch forces. This revelation beckoned to the historian's insatiable curiosity.

With bated breath, Dr. Blackthorn gently opened the Canticles, its pages crackling with the weight of forgotten prophecies. The arcane language within told of cosmic entities that stirred in the shadows, waiting to be awakened by the festive cheer of Christmas celebrations. At that moment, amidst the forgotten tomes and the hushed corridors of the library, Dr. Evelyn Blackthorn stumbled upon a cosmic revelation. This discovery would set the intricate dance between the ordinary and the eldritch across the twelve nights of Yule.

As Dr. Evelyn Blackthorn delicately flipped through the pages of the Canticles of Yule, the ancient tome exuded an eldritch aura that hung palpably in the air. The words within seemed to come alive, resonating with cosmic energies that whispered of Yuletide prophecies dating back centuries.

The atmosphere in the forgotten library shifted as if attuned to the revelations within the Canticles. Eldritch energies emanated from the pages, weaving an unseen tapestry that bridged the mundane with the cosmic unknown. Her eyes scanning the arcane script, Dr. Blackthorn felt the touch of cosmic forces that transcended the boundaries of ordinary perception.

With each turned page, the eldritch aura intensified, carrying whispers of ancient celebrations and cosmic entities entwined in a dance through the ages. The Canticles, a vessel of heavenly revelations, resonated with the festive cheer of Christmas, unveiling a prophecy that connected the threads of Yuletide merriment with the eldritch mysteries that lurked beyond.

In that quiet moment, within the sanctum of the forgotten library, Dr. Evelyn Blackthorn became a conduit between worlds. The eldritch energies flowed through her, igniting a curiosity that transcended the boundaries of scholarly pursuit. Once dormant in the dusty shelves, the Canticles now pulsed with a cosmic heartbeat, inviting her to unravel the secrets hidden within its pages.

As the eldritch aura enveloped her, Dr. Blackthorn's journey through the Canticles unfolded not merely as an exploration of ancient prophecies but as a communion with forces that blurred the line between the festive spirit of Yule and the cosmic mysteries that awaited revelation. The forgotten tome, now awakened, held the promise of an odyssey where the ordinary and the eldritch danced in harmony across the twelve nights of Yule.

As Dr. Evelyn Blackthorn delved into the cryptic passages of the Canticles of Yule, a revelation unfurled before her discerning eyes. Once shrouded in mystery, the arcane script yielded its secrets to her scholarly gaze. In the quiet confines of the forgotten library, she deciphered the ancient language, realizing that the Canticles unveiled a cosmic prophecy. This tapestry foretold the merging of Christmas celebrations and eldritch entities.

As the puzzle pieces fell into place, Dr. Blackthorn saw the threads of Yuletide joy intricately woven with the cosmic dread that lurked beyond the veil of reality. The revelation transcended the ordinary understanding of festive cheer, presenting a cosmic dance where the merriment of Christmas celebrations catalyzed the awakening of eldritch forces.

The Canticles spoke of a cosmic convergence when the boundaries between the festive and the cosmic would thin. In her deciphering, Dr. Blackthorn understood that the prophecy outlined a dance of intertwining destinies—those who reveled in the mirth of Christmas unknowingly becoming conduits for the eldritch energies that stirred in the shadows.

In illuminating her scholarly understanding, Dr. Blackthorn grasped the significance of the revelation. Once silent witnesses to centuries of Yuletide celebrations, the Canticles held the key to a cosmic symphony that would unfold across the twelve nights of Yule. The ancient prophecy foretold a mingling of worlds, where the mundane and the cosmic would converge in an intricate dance. This revelation beckoned Dr. Blackthorn into a journey that transcended the realms of academic pursuit and ventured into the cosmic unknown.

As Dr. Evelyn Blackthorn immersed herself in the revelations of the Canticles of Yule, a presence materialized at a pivotal moment—a figure draped in mystery and knowledge. Professor Nathaniel Eldritch emerged from the shadowy recesses of the forgotten library, his arrival coinciding with the unfolding cosmic tale within the ancient tome.

Professor Eldritch, the guardian of arcane secrets, cast a cryptic gaze upon Dr. Blackthorn. His silhouette, etched against the flickering candlelight, bore the weight of untold knowledge. With an enigmatic demeanor, he approached, his steps echoing like whispers through the dim-lit corridors.

In the shared silence of scholar and librarian, Professor Eldritch intervened at the precise moment when the revelations within the Canticles took an intricate turn. His words, cryptic and laden with cosmic significance, guided Dr. Blackthorn through the labyrinth of Eldritch's prophecies. The librarian's insight became a lantern in the cosmic darkness, illuminating the path through the arcane passages that spoke of the merging of Christmas celebrations and eldritch entities.

As Professor Eldritch guided her, the questions lingering in Dr. Blackthorn's mind deepened. The librarian's cryptic demeanor made her ponder his role in the cosmic symphony foretold by the Canticles. Was he merely a custodian of knowledge, or did his presence signify a more profound connection to the unfolding cosmic tale?

In that moment of scholarly communion, Dr. Blackthorn and Professor Eldritch intertwined in the dance of revelation. Once a silent witness, the ancient tome now echoed with their shared understanding. The librarian's intervention added complexity to the unfolding cosmic tale, leaving lingering questions that beckoned the scholar to delve deeper into the mysteries beyond the pages of the Canticles of Yule.

As the ancient pages of the Canticles of Yule turned into the forgotten library, a sense of foreboding hung in the air. Dr. Evelyn Blackthorn, guided by the cryptic wisdom of Professor Nathaniel Eldritch, found herself at the threshold of a cosmic revelation. The eldritch energies whispered secrets that transcended the boundaries of festive joy, and the librarian's intervention had woven her destiny into the cosmic tapestry foretold by the Canticles.

In the closing moments of this introduction, an unspoken pact unfolded—a covenant forged between Dr. Blackthorn and the cosmic forces awakened within the pages. The air, thick with the eldritch aura, resonated with the weight of a destiny that reached beyond the mundane celebrations of Christmas.

The closing impression left a lingering sense of anticipation and trepidation. The scholarly pursuit that began with the discovery of the Canticles transformed into a pact with cosmic forces that transcended the ordinary understanding of Yuletide merriment. Now bound to the revelations within the ancient tome, Dr. Blackthorn stood at the crossroads of an eldritch web. In this tapestry, the destinies of celebrants and eldritch entities became intricately entwined.

This introduction concluded not with finality but with the resonance of cosmic mysteries awaiting revelation. The stage was set, and the closing impression left an indelible mark—a prelude to the twelve nights of Yule, where the ordinary and the eldritch would dance in a symphony of cosmic proportions. The forgotten library, now steeped in the echoes of revelations, stood as a portal to a cosmic journey. B bound by the pact, Dr. Evelyn Blackthorn awaited the unraveling of the eldritch tale that would unfold across the twelve nights of Eldritch Yule.

The Yuletide Beacon

The air buzzed with anticipation in the heart of the coastal town, where whitewashed cottages adorned with twinkling lights formed a quaint tapestry. The salty scent of the sea mingled with the aroma of holiday treats as the townsfolk prepared for the imminent Christmas festivities. The town square, a bustling hub of activity, was a canvas painted with the hues of festive decorations and the joyful chatter of those caught in the spirit of Yule.

Dominating the scene, an iconic lighthouse stood proudly atop the cliff, its silhouette outlined against the darkening sky. The imposing structure, a beacon of maritime safety, held a timeless allure that transcended its practical purpose. As the sun dipped below the horizon, the lighthouse came to life, its beam reaching out into the vast expanse of the ocean.

Unbeknownst to the celebrants below, the radiant glow of the Yuletide beacon cast more than just light across the waves. Deep within the cosmic unknown, ancient entities stirred, drawn by the luminous invitation that stretched beyond the mundane purpose of guiding ships safely to shore. The iconic lighthouse, an unwitting accomplice in the cosmic tale of Eldritch Yule, stood as a symbol of festive cheer and unwittingly beckoned forces from realms beyond, setting the stage for the first night of the cosmic symphony.

In the coastal town, Captain Henry Meriwether, a weathered lighthouse keeper, stood as a stalwart pillar of the community. His face bore the etchings of countless nights spent tending to the beacon that crowned the cliff. Known for his unwavering dedication to keeping the lighthouse aflame, Captain Meriwether was not merely a guardian of maritime safety but a symbol of resilience in the face of the relentless sea.

Beside him, his daughter, Sarah Meriwether, embodied the spirit of the coastal town with her youthful enthusiasm. Beneath her lively exterior, however, lurked an innate connection to the cosmic unknown. This link defied the boundaries of the mundane. Her curious gaze often wandered beyond the horizon, drawn by forces that eluded the perception of those immersed in the daily rhythm of coastal life.

As preparations for Christmas unfolded in the town square, Captain Meriwether's weathered hands meticulously tended to the lighthouse, ensuring its beam would pierce the night with unwavering strength. Standing sentinel on the cliff, the iconic structure held secrets unbeknownst to the celebrants below—a beacon not just for seafarers but an unwitting summoner of cosmic forces.

His daughter Sarah moved through the festive atmosphere with a blend of youthful exuberance and a quiet knowing. In her eyes, the twinkling lights mirrored the distant stars, and the joyous carols carried whispers of cosmic melodies. Unbeknownst to the townsfolk, the Meriwethers, in their roles as keepers of the coastal flame, were destined to become participants in a cosmic dance—a familial link to the eldritch forces that responded to the Yuletide beacon's luminous call. The stage was set, and as the coastal town prepared for Christmas, the cosmic forces stirred, drawn by the connection between the Meriwethers and the unfolding mysteries of Eldritch Yule.

In the coastal town, the figure of Captain Henry Meriwether emerged as a living embodiment of the lighthouse's enduring legacy. Weathered by the sea's relentless embrace, Captain Meriwether upheld a routine etched in the maritime history of his family. The Meriwethers, a lineage intertwined with the beacon's purpose, had become custodians of a connection that stretched beyond the practicality of guiding ships.

The routine of Captain Meriwether unfolded with a stoic dedication that mirrored the rhythmic cadence of the waves. With each step up the spiraling staircase, he ascended towards the crown of the lighthouse, a space where the sea's vast expanse met the celestial dome. The keeper of the Yuletide beacon, Captain Meriwether's hands moved with a familiarity born of countless nights spent nurturing the luminous guide that overlooked the coastal town.

As he tended to the lantern, the flickering glow illuminated his weathered features—the lines etched by winds, salt spray, and eyes that held the wisdom of maritime tales. The routine extended beyond the mechanical workings of the lighthouse; it embodied a familial commitment passed down through generations, a sacred duty that resonated with the essence of Yuletide traditions.

Captain Meriwether's stoic dedication to the Yuletide beacon carried echoes of familial lore. This legacy transcended the tangible duty of maintaining the light. Beneath the exterior of routine and tradition lay a connection to unspoken cosmic forces. This heritage destined the Meriwethers to become unwitting participants in the cosmic tapestry of Eldritch Yule. The coastal town, nestled below the guardian lighthouse, stood as a testament to the enduring link between the Meriwethers and the cosmic mysteries that awaited revelation on this first night of Yule.

In the coastal town, the arrival of Yule heralded a transformation as the community burst into vibrant life. Festive preparations infused every corner with an energy that transcended the mundane routines of daily existence. The marketplace, once a tranquil gathering place, now teemed with activity as merchants adorned stalls with seasonal wares, their festive offerings mirroring the radiant spirit of the season.

With voices tuned to the melody of holiday cheer, Carolers rehearsed in the winding streets. The harmonious notes resonated through the air, intertwining with the lively chatter of townsfolk preparing for the upcoming celebrations. Each lyric carried the promise of joy, yet unbeknownst to the carolers, their melodies would awaken more than just the festive spirit.

As the sun dipped below the horizon, casting hues of gold and crimson over the coastal town, the aroma of holiday treats wafted through the air. Bakeries and kitchens became alchemical workshops, conjuring delights that spoke to the heart of Yuletide traditions. The scent of spiced cookies, warm cider, and roasted chestnuts mingled with the crisp sea breeze, creating an olfactory tapestry that enveloped the celebrants in a sensory embrace.

The coastal town transformed into a living canvas in the twilight glow—a tableau of festive joy.

The hustle and bustle mirrored the cosmic forces stirring in response to the Yuletide beacon. Unbeknownst to the townsfolk immersed in the merriment, the preparations for Christmas served as a prelude to a cosmic dance—a symphony of festivities that resonated not only in the hearts of celebrants but also in the cosmic unknown that awaited its role in the unfolding nights of Eldritch Yule.

Intrigued by the secrets whispered in the coastal winds, Sarah Meriwether, the lighthouse keeper's daughter, felt an irresistible pull to embark on a journey into the nooks and crannies of the town. Guided by an unspoken intuition, she meandered through the winding streets, her curious wanderings taking her beyond the well-trodden paths of festive revelry.

Sarah's perceptive gaze, fueled by a connection to the cosmic unknown, discerned patterns in the decorations that seemed to defy the ordinary. Twinkling lights formed constellations, wreaths held arrangements resembling celestial maps, and even the snowflakes on storefronts mirrored the intricate geometry of eldritch sigils. The coastal winds, carrying whispers of cosmic mysteries, guided Sarah's steps toward the convergence of festive joy and otherworldly secrets.

Inadvertently stumbling upon these cryptic symbols, Sarah's curious wanderings wove her into the intricate tapestry of Eldritch Yule. The symbols, hidden in plain sight, beckoned to her innate connection with the cosmic unknown, setting the stage for a revelation that would transcend the ordinary bounds of Yuletide merriment. As the coastal town pulsed with festive energy, Sarah's unwitting discovery began a cosmic dance that awaited its cues from the Yuletide beacon and the eldritch forces it summoned.

As Christmas Eve approached, the coastal town buzzed with anticipation, and the culmination of festive preparations drew near. The heart of the celebration lay in the annual illumination of the lighthouse. This event transcended the bounds of tradition and carried cosmic significance unbeknownst to the gathered townsfolk.

The Lighthouse Illumination Ceremony drew the community together, creating a shared space where the festive spirit harmonized with the cosmic energies stirred by the Yuletide beacon. Families and friends assembled near the iconic structure, their faces aglow with the warmth of holiday cheer. Standing tall and majestic against the night sky, the lighthouse became the focal point of the communal celebration.

As the appointed hour neared, Captain Henry Meriwether, his weathered features illuminated by the glow of the Yuletide beacon, took center stage. His steady hands kindled the flame within the lantern, marking the ceremonial ignition that heralded the climax of Christmas Eve festivities. The radiant light emanating from the lighthouse cast a luminous aura over the gathered townsfolk, uniting them in a moment of shared wonder.

Unbeknownst to the celebrants, the illumination of the lighthouse served a dual purpose. Beyond its role as a beacon for maritime safety, the festive tradition unwittingly resonated with cosmic significance. The radiant glow reached into the cosmic unknown, signaling to eldritch forces that the time had come for the cosmic dance to unfold.

As the coastal town basked in the luminosity of the Yuletide beacon, a subtle shift occurred in the fabric of reality. The cosmic forces, attuned to the festive celebration, stirred in response to the ceremonial illumination. The annual tradition, veiled in the guise of Christmas joy, catalyzed the convergence of realms. This phenomenon would begin a series of cosmic revelations across the twelve nights of Eldritch Yule.

As Captain Henry Meriwether kindled the Yuletide beacon during the Lighthouse Illumination

Ceremony, a seemingly ordinary act sent cosmic ripples reverberating through the unseen realms. The radiant glow, symbolic of festive tradition, became a catalyst that awakened ancient forces lying dormant beneath the waves of the cosmic unknown.

Unbeknownst to the celebrants gathered around the lighthouse, the act of kindling the Yuletide beacon was a key. This resonant note echoed through the fabric of reality. In the unseen realms, where eldritch forces slumbered, the cosmic ripples stirred dormant energies, signaling a moment of celestial alignment. The luminous beacon, fueled by the festive spirit of Christmas, became a conduit through which the eldritch entities responded to the cosmic call.

Beneath the surface of the ocean waves, where shadows and mysteries intertwined, the cosmic ripples manifested as undulating currents of otherworldly energies. Ancient forces, stirred from their slumber, sensed the luminosity piercing the veil between realms. Like tendrils reaching out from the depths, the eldritch entities responded to the Yuletide beacon, drawn by the convergence of festive joy and cosmic revelation.

The cosmic ripples, imperceptible to the celebrants, marked the initiation of a cosmic dance that transcended the boundaries of the ordinary. As the Yuletide beacon continued to cast its radiant glow over the coastal town, the unseen realms responded with an awakening that set the stage for the mysteries yet to unfold across the twelve nights of Eldritch Yule.

The coastal town underwent a subtle but palpable transformation, with the Yuletide beacon ablaze. Invisible threads, woven by an eldritch presence, began to materialize in the atmosphere, creating connections that bridged the gap between the celebratory haven and the cosmic unknown.

Once filled with the harmonious notes of carolers and the scent of festive treats, the air now carried an ethereal quality—a whisper of unseen energies that danced through the unseen threads. The cosmic ripples, initiated by the kindling of the Yuletide beacon, manifested as an eldritch undercurrent, infusing the atmosphere with a subtle tension.

Unbeknownst to the celebrants, the invisible threads stretched beyond the confines of the coastal town, reaching into realms where ancient forces stirred in response to the cosmic call. Like tendrils of cosmic fabric, these threads wove intricate patterns that connected festive decorations, lighthouse beams, and the unsuspecting townsfolk to the cosmic unknown.

The coastal town became a focal point as the eldritch presence threaded through the unseen realms. In this nexus, the festive spirit of Christmas is seamlessly intertwined with cosmic energies. The shift in the atmosphere, imperceptible to ordinary senses, heralded the beginning of a cosmic symphony, where the invisible threads would guide the destinies of those caught in the eldritch dance.

The townsfolk continued their merriment in the coastal haven, unaware of the cosmic forces entwining with the Yuletide festivities. Little did they know that the invisible threads, woven with eldritch precision, marked the commencement of a journey into the cosmic unknown—a trip that awaited revelation as the nights of Eldritch Yule unfolded.

Captain Henry Meriwether, attuned to the hidden currents of the sea and the cosmic forces beyond, felt an unsettling shift in the air as he tended to the lighthouse. Amidst the festive ambiance and the radiant glow of the Yuletide beacon, an inner turmoil gripped him—an unspoken awareness of the unseen forces stirring in the cosmic unknown.

As his weathered hands meticulously tended to the lantern, Captain Meriwether's senses, finely tuned by years spent navigating the maritime mysteries, detected a subtle disturbance in the atmospheric currents. The gentle caress of the coastal winds carried a different cadence, a whisper of cosmic energies intermingling with the sea's familiar song.

A gnawing sense of foreboding settled upon Captain Meriwether's shoulders. This weight mirrored the unseen burdens borne by the lighthouse keeper's lineage. The connection passed down through generations resonated with the captain's innate understanding of the mystical ties between the Yuletide beacon and the eldritch forces.

As the luminous glow extended its reach into the unseen realms, Captain Meriwether couldn't shake the feeling that the act of kindling the Yuletide beacon had consequences beyond the visible horizon. The inner turmoil mirrored the clash between the responsibilities of a lighthouse keeper and the awareness of cosmic forces responding to the festive call.

Despite the festive revelry surrounding him, Captain Meriwether, a guardian of maritime safety and unwitting participant in the cosmic dance, stood at the intersection of tradition and the unknown. His gnawing sense of foreboding became a silent harbinger of the cosmic revelations yet to unfold across the twelve nights of Eldritch Yule.

As the Yuletide beacon cast its luminous glow over the coastal town, a mysterious presence observed the festivities from the ocean's depths. This otherworldly observer, whose gaze transcended mortal comprehension, watched as the city was filled with merriment and cheer. From the shadows and mysteries of the ocean, the presence silently bore witness to the joyous occasion.

The unseen observer, attuned to the cosmic currents that rippled through the unseen realms, beheld the vibrant tapestry of Yuletide joy interwoven with the subtle threads of eldritch energies. The coastal town, aglow with festive lights and resonant with holiday cheer, became a tableau viewed through the enigmatic eyes of the cosmic unknown.

From the abyssal depths, the unseen observer witnessed the inner turmoil of Captain Henry Meriwether, the weaving of invisible threads connecting the celebrants to the cosmic unknown, and the eldritch forces responding to the Yuletide beacon. A cosmic dance, set against the backdrop of Christmas festivities, unfolded before the observer's gaze.

This silent observer, whose motives and nature remained in cosmic mystery, foreshadowed the revelations that would unfold in the coming nights. From the depths of the oceanic abyss, the cosmic observer became a silent witness to the convergence of realms—a prelude to the cosmic symphony that would mark the twelve nights of Eldritch Yule with celestial wonder and dread.

The Enchanted Ornaments

The opulent Harrington Manor was a beacon of elegance amid the wintry landscape. Its grandiose halls adorned with twinkling lights reflected the affluence of the Harrington family, setting the stage for the second night of Eldritch Yule.

A mysterious workshop hid in plain sight within the manor's sprawling expanse. Shrouded in an air of craftsmanship and mystique, this hidden enclave played host to the arcane artistry of Beatrice Wrenfield. The Artisan's Workshop, concealed behind rich tapestries and ornate furnishings, became the nexus where enchantment met craftsmanship.

As guests reveled in the festive ambiance of Harrington Manor, they remained unaware of the arcane currents flowing beneath the surface. The luxurious setting masked the subtle dance of eldritch energies in the secretive workshop, where Beatrice Wrenfield practiced her otherworldly art.

The manor's halls echoed with celebrants' laughter, and the Yuletide beacon's enchanting glow cast a luminous aura over the opulent surroundings. Yet, unbeknownst to the revelers, the Artisan's Workshop held secrets that would intertwine the beauty of craftsmanship with the eldritch mysteries of the cosmos.

In the heart of Harrington Manor, the stage was set for a tale that blended the season's splendor with the enchantment of arcane arts. The second night of Eldritch Yule awaited, its secrets veiled within the luxurious halls and the hidden workshop where Beatrice Wrenfield wove spells that would leave an indelible mark on the festivities to come.

Emily Harrington, the young heiress of Harrington Manor, moved through the opulent halls with an air of grace. Captivated by the allure of the mysterious ornaments that adorned the manor, she navigated the festivities with an insatiable curiosity that mirrored her fascination with the unknown.

Amid the celebration, Professor Jonathan Ward, an ornithologist with an academic interest in the arcane, was drawn to Harrington Manor. The peculiar symbols adorning the enchanting ornaments had piqued his scholarly curiosity, guiding him to the heart of the Eldritch Yule festivities.

Beatrice Wrenfield, a skilled artisan with otherworldly talent, stood at the nexus of mystery and craftsmanship. Known for crafting enchanted objects that blurred the boundaries between the mundane and the cosmic, Beatrice's presence in the Artisan's Workshop added an element of intrigue to the unfolding night.

As Emily Harrington explored the opulence of her ancestral home, Professor Jonathan Ward delved into the symbolism etched into the mysterious ornaments. Meanwhile, Beatrice Wrenfield continued her arcane work, weaving spells into the fabric of the enchanting decorations that adorned Harrington Manor.

The convergence of Emily's curiosity, Professor Ward's academic inquiry, and Beatrice's mystical craftsmanship set the stage for a night where the mundane and cosmic boundaries would blur. The second night of Eldritch Yule unfolded with a trio of key players, each unknowingly contributing to a tale that transcended the elegance of Harrington Manor and delved into the mysteries hidden within the Artisan's Workshop.

In the heart of Eldritch Yule's second night, readers are transported into the lavish splendor of Harrington Manor. Gilded halls adorned with twinkling lights and towering Christmas trees created an atmosphere of opulence and festivity. Elegance and mystery intertwined as guests reveled in the festive ambiance, oblivious to the arcane currents flowing beneath the surface.

The manor's grandeur, a testament to the Harrington family's affluence, became a canvas upon which the eldritch mysteries of the night unfolded. Lavish tapestries and rich furnishings provided the backdrop for a celebration that masked the subtle dance of cosmic energies at play.

The air seemed to shimmer with enchantment as guests mingled in the opulent surroundings. The Yuletide beacon's glow extended into every corner of Harrington Manor, casting a luminous aura over the festivities. Elegance and mystery became synonymous, concealing the secrets hidden within the Artisan's Workshop.

It was a night where the opulence of the setting masked the cosmic tapestry being woven in the hidden alcoves of the manor. Amidst the gilded splendor and the revelry of the celebrants, the second night of Eldritch Yule unfolded, promising an exploration of the unknown that would leave an indelible mark on the tales to come.

In the luminous halls of Harrington Manor, Emily Harrington, the heiress to the estate, found herself captivated by the mysterious ornaments that had adorned her family's home for generations. The allure of these enigmatic decorations stirred her curiosity, setting in motion a quest to unravel the secrets they held.

Intricately crafted and rich with symbolism, the ornaments whispered tales of untold mysteries to Emily's keen senses. As the heiress moved through the opulent surroundings, her steps guided by the cosmic currents of Eldritch Yule, the ornaments beckoned her with a silent invitation to delve into the arcane secrets concealed within their ornate designs.

Emily's curiosity, a flame fueled by a family history intertwined with eldritch mysteries, led her to explore the hidden corners of Harrington Manor. With each step, she ventured deeper into the heart of the opulence that surrounded her, the mysterious ornaments becoming a trail of breadcrumbs guiding her toward the secrets that awaited discovery.

Amidst the festive celebration, Emily's quest unfolded, driven by an insatiable desire to understand the significance of the ornaments that had graced Harrington Manor through generations. The heiress' curiosity became a crucial element in the cosmic dance of the second night of Eldritch Yule, as the secrets hidden within the decorations awaited revelation, setting the stage for a tale that blurred the boundaries between family legacy and cosmic destiny.

In the tapestry of Harrington Manor's second night, Professor Jonathan Ward, an ornithologist with a scholarly penchant for the arcane, found himself drawn to the estate. The mysterious symbols adorning the ornaments, intricately intertwined with avian motifs, had ignited his academic curiosity, leading him to investigate the mystical connection between these symbols and the eldritch energies that permeated the manor.

Arriving at Harrington Manor with scholarly anticipation, Professor Ward stepped into the opulent surroundings that masked the cosmic currents. The enchanting decorations, each imbued with arcane significance, seemed to beckon the ornithologist, their symbols forming a cryptic language that spoke of untold cosmic secrets.

As Professor Ward delved into the intricacies of the avian motifs, he felt a resonance with the unseen forces that stirred within the manor. The connection between the symbols and Eldritch's energies became apparent, and the ornithologist's pursuit of knowledge seamlessly merged with the cosmic revelations of Eldritch Yule's second night.

Within the gilded halls, the ornithologist's arrival added another layer to the cosmic dance unfolding at Harrington Manor. The symbols on the ornaments held the promise of arcane wisdom. Professor Ward's investigation became a crucial thread in the intricate tapestry of the night, linking the scholarly pursuit of avian mysteries to the cosmic wonders hidden within the enchanted decorations.

The veil of mystery surrounding Harrington Manor's second night lifted as the door to Beatrice Wrenfield's workshop swung open. An arcane atelier was revealed before Emily Harrington and Professor Jonathan Ward, a hidden realm within the opulent estate overflowing with curious artifacts, half-finished creations, and the lingering scent of mystical incense.

The Artisan's Workshop, concealed behind layers of opulence and elegance, became a sanctuary for Beatrice's otherworldly craft. It was a place where the boundaries between the mundane and the cosmic blurred, and the air crackled with the energy of eldritch enchantment. The curious artifacts adorned the workshop's shelves seemed to pulse with unseen forces, each a testament to Beatrice's mastery over the arcane.

As Emily and Professor Ward stepped into the workshop, they found themselves surrounded by the tools of Beatrice's trade—arcane symbols, enchanted materials, and the subtle hum of cosmic energies interwoven with the very fabric of the creations. The half-finished artifacts hinted at the meticulous craftsmanship that went into each piece, each one a bridge between the mundane and the mystical.

In the heart of the Artisan's Workshop, secrets awaited discovery. The unveiling of this hidden realm marked a pivotal moment in the cosmic dance of Eldritch Yule's second night. Within the confines of the workshop, Beatrice Wrenfield's craft would intertwine with the unfolding mysteries of Emily's family legacy and Professor Ward's scholarly pursuit, setting the stage for a night where the boundaries of reality and the cosmic unknown would continue to blur.

As Emily and Professor Ward delved into the secrets of Beatrice Wrenfield's Artisan's Workshop, they uncovered a revelation that would forever alter their perception of the mysterious ornaments. Each ornament, carefully crafted with arcane precision, possessed an otherworldly allure that transcended the boundaries of traditional craftsmanship.

In the dim light of the workshop, Emily and Professor Ward marveled at the intricate details of the ornaments. Once seen as mere decorations, the symbols now revealed themselves as conduits to cosmic forces. The craftsmanship, infused with eldritch energies, hinted at a connection that surpassed the limits of mortal understanding.

As they examined the ornaments, the duo felt a subtle resonance with the cosmic currents that wove through Harrington Manor. The enchantment within each piece seemed to respond to the unseen forces that pulsed through the air, creating an ethereal symphony that echoed the cosmic dance of Eldritch Yule's second night.

The discovery of the ornaments' otherworldly allure marked a turning point in the tale. Emily and Professor Ward stood at the nexus of traditional craftsmanship and cosmic enchantment, their understanding of the night's mysteries deepening as they embraced the cosmic connection that linked the opulence of Harrington Manor to the eldritch unknown. The second night of Eldritch Yule continued to unfold, revealing layers of enchantment that beckoned the protagonists further into the cosmic tapestry of intertwined destinies.

Within the grandeur of Harrington Manor, Emily and Professor Ward found themselves immersed in the secrets of the ornaments, and with each revelation, the elegance of the estate underwent a subtle transformation. What was once considered mundane became a canvas for the eldritch to weave its cosmic threads.

The gilded halls, adorned with twinkling lights and towering Christmas trees, now resonated with the subtle hum of mystical energies. The opulence of Harrington Manor, once a testament to earthly wealth, became a backdrop for the infusion of the eldritch unknown. The air seemed to shimmer with the unseen forces at play, turning the estate into a stage where the cosmic dance unfolded.

As Emily and Professor Ward moved through the transformed manor, they witnessed the fusion of traditional Yuletide splendor and cosmic enchantment. The once-static decorations now pulsed with eldritch vitality, and the earthly and the otherworldly boundaries blurred with each passing moment.

The subtle transformation became a visual manifestation of the cosmic currents that guided the second night of Eldritch Yule. Harrington Manor, a stage for the unfolding mysteries, bore witness to the intermingling of the mundane and the eldritch, setting the tone for a night where traditional elegance and cosmic wonder would coalesce in a dance that transcended the boundaries of the known and the unknown.

In the heart of Harrington Manor's transformed splendor, Emily and Professor Ward sought guidance from the enigmatic artisan Beatrice Wrenfield. As they approached her within the Artisan's Workshop, Beatrice, draped in an air of mystery, acknowledged their inquisitive gazes with a knowing smile.

With a sweep of her hand, Beatrice gestured to the array of enchanted ornaments, each emanating an ethereal glow. Her words carried a weight of cryptic wisdom as she revealed the cosmic energies woven into her creations. She explained that the symbols etched on the ornaments were a language that connected the earthly with the eldritch, inviting the cosmic unknown into the realm of tradition.

However, Beatrice's guidance came with a subtle warning—the potential consequences of meddling with the eldritch. As she spoke, the artisan's eyes flickered with a glimpse of cosmic understanding, hinting at the delicate balance between the enchantment of Yuletide and the unfathomable depths of cosmic dread.

In the presence of Beatrice Wrenfield, Emily and Professor Ward grappled with the realization that their pursuit of knowledge and unraveling cosmic mysteries carried weighty implications. The artisan's revelation marked a pivotal moment in the night, where the line between curiosity and caution blurred, and the protagonists faced a choice that would shape the cosmic tapestry of Eldritch Yule's second night.

As Beatrice Wrenfield continued her cryptic guidance, she spoke of interconnected realms woven together by eldritch energies. The enchanting ornaments, symbols of tradition and cosmic enchantment, served as conduits to realms beyond human comprehension. Emily and Professor Ward, caught in the delicate dance between curiosity and caution, listened intently as Beatrice unveiled the unseen threads that connected their world to cosmic dimensions.

Once a haven of earthly craftsmanship, the Artisan's Workshop transformed into a nexus where the boundaries between realms blurred. The symbols on the ornaments resonated with cosmic vibrations, creating a tapestry that bridged the known and the unknown. The air itself became charged with the essence of interconnected realms as if the very fabric of reality undulated with the cosmic energies unveiled by Beatrice.

Emily and Professor Ward, now aware of the delicate balance between tradition and the eldritch, found themselves entangled in the intricate web of interconnected realms. The second night of Eldritch Yule unfolded with the realization that their actions reverberated through the opulence of Harrington Manor and the unseen dimensions that responded to the cosmic call of Yuletide enchantment.

As the night unfolded within Harrington Manor, the mystique deepened, shrouding Emily, Professor Ward, and all those unsuspecting in an atmosphere of uncertainty. The once ornate ornaments, now pulsating with eldritch energies, emanated an otherworldly glow, foreshadowing an imminent cosmic revelation.

Observing the unfolding events with a discerning gaze, Beatrice Wrenfield witnessed the protagonists grapple with the profound implications of their discoveries. Symbols, once a language of aesthetic allure, now murmured cosmic secrets resonating with dimensions unseen.

Within the confines of the Artisan's Workshop, the air became charged with anticipation. As this phase of the night drew to a close, Emily and Professor Ward found themselves standing at the precipice of a cosmic unveiling. The boundary between beauty and terror blurred, and the mysteries unraveled in the opulent halls of Harrington Manor hinted at a night where Yuletide enchantment and the cosmic unknown would entwine, ushering them towards the third night of Eldritch Yule—a night cloaked in the eldritch wonders awaiting discovery.

The wintry night enchanted the village square in the heart of Frostbitten Carols. The air crackled with the season's magic, and the twinkling lights adorned every corner, transforming the square into a luminous haven. A towering Christmas tree stood proudly, its branches laden with shimmering ornaments that caught the glow of the festive lights. Laughter echoed through the air as villagers, bundled in scarves and coats, reveled in the warmth of camaraderie and the upbeat melodies that wafted through the chilly night.

The snow-kissed carolers, a spirited ensemble adorned in a tapestry of colors, gathered at the heart of the square. Their breath formed misty clouds in the cold air, adding an ethereal quality to the scene. The anticipation was palpable as they prepared to embark on their festive journey. The route they would take wound through the village's quaint streets, a labyrinth of charming houses and frost-laden trees that created a picturesque setting for their joyful serenade.

The frost-laden trees, their branches delicately coated in a shimmering layer of ice, stood like sentinels, witnessing the ageless ritual of carolers braving the wintry night. Each step of the carolers left imprints in the freshly fallen snow, marking a path that led through the heart of the village. The radiant glow of the Christmas lights illuminated the route, turning it into a magical trail that beckoned all to join in the festive celebration.

The carolers, led by the village's most spirited singers, began their journey beneath archways of frost-laden branches. Their voices, a harmonious blend of tradition and merriment, echoed through the town, infusing the air with the timeless tunes of the season. Villagers, drawn from their homes by the irresistible melodies, followed the procession, their faces aglow with the spirit of togetherness.

Unbeknownst to the villagers, the joyous carols resonated with a cosmic energy that transcended the ordinary. While seemingly rooted in tradition, the festive celebration carried a resonance that reached beyond the veil of the mundane. Eldritch forces stirred in the unseen corners of the cosmic tapestry, responding to the harmonies that bridged the gap between the earthly and the unknown.

As the villagers continued their journey through the snow-kissed streets, the third night of Eldritch Yule unfolded its mysteries. The enchanting melodies became a conduit, inviting the cosmic forces to dance within the harmonies of the season. The air crackled with unseen energies, and the villagers, immersed in the warmth of community and celebration, unwittingly participated in a dance between festive carols and the eldritch wonders that awaited their awakening.

Clara Whitman, the heart and soul of the caroling ensemble, stepped forward into the frostbitten night, her breath forming a halo in the chilly air. With a voice that echoed like a joyous bell, she led the carolers through the village square, her enthusiasm contagious. Clara's presence exuded the very essence of Christmas. As she sang, the villagers couldn't help but be drawn into the enchantment that emanated from her.

A skilled violinist, Thomas Hayes, accompanied the carolers with melodic strains that resonated through the wintry air. His fingers danced over the strings, producing harmonies that intertwined with Clara's vocals, creating a symphony that elevated the festive atmosphere. There was an unspoken connection between Thomas and the cosmic energies lying dormant. This connection transcended the ordinary notes of a violin and hinted at a deeper, otherworldly resonance.

Clara's voice soared as the duo led the carolers along the snow-kissed route, and Thomas's violin responded in kind. The village came alive with the magical strains, the frost-laden trees standing witness to the cosmic dance unfolding beneath their branches. Clara's boundless enthusiasm infected the villagers, and soon, the entire procession became a moving tapestry of joy, music, and cosmic energies.

Unbeknownst to Clara, Thomas, and the villagers, their harmonious celebration had become a beacon for the eldritch forces that lingered in the cosmic shadows. The unseen observers, drawn by the celestial cadence of the carols, began to stir in the cosmic tapestry. Clara's voice and Thomas's violin had become conduits, channels through which the festive merriment reached into the realms beyond, blurring the earthly and cosmic boundaries.

As the night deepened and the villagers continued their journey, the cosmic energies responded to the festive call, weaving unseen threads that connected the joyous celebration to the mysteries of Eldritch Yule. Clara's voice, resonating with the spirit of Christmas, became a vessel for the eldritch forces to infuse the night with an enchantment that transcended tradition. The third night unfolded, and with each note sung and played, the cosmic dance between the carolers and the unknown intensified, setting the stage for the cosmic revelations that awaited the village in the nights to come.

The village square lay nestled beneath a blanket of freshly fallen snow, transformed into the heart of festivities as the winter night cast its enchanting spell. Twinkling lights adorned the trees, glowing warmly over the snow-laden ground. The towering Christmas tree stood proudly at the center, its branches adorned with an array of ornaments, each telling a story of holiday cheer.

The air was filled with the laughter of children building snowmen, the aroma of roasted chestnuts wafting from street vendors, and the joyous chatter of villagers exchanging heartfelt greetings. The village square was a canvas painted with vibrant celebration hues, every corner adorned with decorations that mirrored the cosmic dance in the unseen realms.

Families strolled through the square, their faces aglow with the festive spirit. Shopkeepers displayed their wares, offering holiday treats and trinkets to passersby. The village square, usually a quaint gathering place, had transformed into a bustling nexus of joy, connecting the community in a shared celebration of Eldritch Yule.

Beneath the twinkling lights, Clara Whitman, the lead caroler, took the stage with her companions. The villagers gathered around, their faces lit up with anticipation. Like a beacon of warmth, Clara's voice resonated through the square, drawing everyone into the heart of the festivities. The cosmic energies, responding to the collective joy, stirred in the background, creating an invisible tapestry that connected the earthly celebration to the cosmic unknown.

As the villagers joined in the merriment, the village square became a focal point for converging cosmic energies. Unseen threads of eldritch power intertwined with the laughter, the music, and the shared moments of celebration. The heart of the village pulsed with cosmic energy that transcended the ordinary, setting the stage for the interplay between the festive hearth and the mysteries of Eldritch Yule.

Clara Whitman's voice echoed through the village square, each note a celestial whisper that resonated with an otherworldly melody. The enchanting strains of her song became a musical prelude, weaving through the festive air and capturing the attention of every villager present. The cosmic energies, responding to the harmony, began to stir beneath the surface of the winter night.

As Clara's voice soared, the unseen currents of eldritch power responded in kind, creating an ethereal symphony that blended seamlessly with the traditional carols. The villagers, enchanted by the celestial prelude, felt a subtle shift in the atmosphere. Unbeknownst to them, the cosmic forces that lay dormant had begun to dance in tandem with the festive melodies.

Thomas Hayes, the skilled violinist accompanying Clara, added his magic to the tapestry. His fingers danced across the strings, coaxing hauntingly beautiful notes that resonated with the cosmic energies present. The fusion of earthly and eldritch harmonies created an intricate interplay, blurring the line between the ordinary and the extraordinary.

The villagers, caught in the spell of the musical prelude, unknowingly became participants in a cosmic performance. Each note promised a revelation, a subtle reminder that Eldritch Yule had woven itself into the very fabric of their celebration. As Clara's song reached its crescendo, the cosmic drama unfolded in the unseen realms, setting the stage for the nights and the cosmic revelations awaiting the village square.

With his violin in hand, Thomas Hayes immersed himself in the cosmic dance of tones. His fingers, guided by an otherworldly intuition, produced notes transcending the mere auditory. As the harmonies flowed, they became more than a musical composition; they became a cosmic invocation.

The cosmic tones, woven into the fabric of the village square, reached beyond the audible spectrum, tapping into realms unseen. The villagers, caught in the festive fervor, felt a subtle vibration beneath the surface of the melodies. Unbeknownst to them, the cosmic forces responded to Thomas's cosmic tones, resonating with an energy that blurred the boundaries between the mundane and the eldritch.

The unseen connection to cosmic forces grew more assertive as Thomas continued to play. The winter air, already charged with the season's magic, became a conduit for energies beyond human comprehension. Clara's celestial voice and Thomas's cosmic tones intertwined, creating a divine symphony that echoed through the village, reaching the ears of those who could hear the eldritch undertones beneath the festive cheer.

In the heart of the festivities, the cosmic energies stirred, weaving their influence into the fabric of the Yuletide celebration. Unaware of the unseen forces at play, the villagers continued to revel in the season's joy, unknowingly becoming part of a cosmic narrative that unfolded with each celestial note and cosmic tone.

The festive procession ventured through the quaint village, Clara Whitman leading the carolers with infectious enthusiasm. The air resonated with their harmonious voices as they navigated the snow-kissed streets. The melodies, fueled by the cosmic tones introduced by Thomas Hayes, took on an ethereal quality that transcended the mere celebration of Christmas.

The villagers, drawn to their doorsteps by the celestial sounds, felt a mysterious warmth in the frosty air. Unseen forces, awakened by the cosmic tones, lingered in the wake of the carolers, following the path of the festive serenade. The snow-laden trees, witness to the cosmic energies, shimmered with an otherworldly glow as the procession moved along the carolers' route.

Clara's voice, now a vessel for eldritch resonance, echoed through the village square, amplifying the cosmic energies that intertwined with the festive cheer. As the carolers continued their journey, the unseen forces manifested subtly—frost patterns on windows formed intricate cosmic symbols, and the twinkling lights took on a celestial brilliance.

Unbeknownst to the carolers, their jubilant procession carried them along a cosmic current, aligning with forces beyond the scope of their understanding. The festive serenade, guided by Clara's celestial voice and Thomas's cosmic tones, became a conduit for eldritch energies, marking the village as a focal point for the unfolding cosmic drama beneath the wintry sky.

The cosmic awakening unfolded beneath the winter sky, concealed by the facade of festive cheer. Clara's celestial beacon voice intertwined with Thomas's ethereal melodies, creating a harmonious blend that echoed through the village. Unbeknownst to the carolers, their joyous songs became a magnetic force, resonating with unseen entities drawn from the cosmic unknown.

The carolers' voices acted as a conduit for eldritch energies as the celestial currents coursed through the wintry air. The cosmic forces, dormant for eons, stirred in response to the harmonious vibrations. Shadows, cast by unseen entities, danced along the edges of the village square, their cosmic presence manifesting in subtle disturbances—whispers in the breeze, shimmering lights, and fleeting glimpses of ethereal figures.

Enchanted by the celestial resonance, the villagers remained oblivious to the cosmic awakening. Now a cosmic rite, the festive procession continued to weave through the village, its path guided by forces beyond mortal comprehension. The carolers, unwitting agents of the cosmic drama, sang with heightened fervor, their voices carrying the weight of eldritch energies that wove an intricate tapestry in the fabric of the winter night.

In the cosmic awakening, the village became a nexus where the mundane and the celestial converged, setting the stage for the unfolding mysteries of Eldritch Yule.

Under the celestial influence of the harmonious procession, the snowfall transformed into an ethereal dance. Each flake, touched by cosmic energies, carried a whisper of eldritch influence. Now blanketed in a frostbitten tapestry, the village square bore witness to a transformation beyond the realms of the ordinary.

The snowflakes, once crystalline and pristine, now shimmered with an otherworldly glow. As they descended from the heavens, the cosmic energy infused within them painted the landscape with hues unseen by mortal eyes. Still immersed in the festive revelry, the villagers remained unaware of the subtle metamorphosis around them.

The frost-laden trees, adorned with twinkling lights, became conduits for the eldritch forces. Once mere ornaments of celebration, the decorations now radiated an eerie luminescence, mirroring the cosmic dance unfolding in the unseen realms. The air hummed with a frostbitten resonance, a melody of eldritch notes harmonizing with the festive tunes.

As the carolers continued their journey, the cosmic transformation intensified. The snowflakes, guided by unseen hands, twirled and pirouetted in a celestial ballet, reflecting the intertwined dance of joy and cosmic revelation. Enchanted by the frostbitten beauty, the villagers reveled in the unknowing embrace of eldritch forces that had become an integral part of their winter celebration.

Amidst the cosmic resonance emanating from his violin, Thomas Hayes felt an unspoken connection with the unseen forces drawn to the carolers' joyous melodies. As his fingers danced over the strings, weaving harmonies transcending the mundane, an intangible link formed between him and the cosmic energies lingering in the winter air.

Thomas, the silent violinist, was no stranger to the mystical undertones woven into the fabric of his music. The notes he produced to bridge the gap between the festive procession and the unseen realms. In the quiet moments between melodies, he sensed a subtle dialogue with forces beyond mortal comprehension. This unspoken exchange left him grappling with the mysteries that enveloped his musical gift.

Enraptured by the ethereal transformation of their winter celebration, the villagers remained oblivious to the cosmic connection deepening within the heart of the festive procession. Thomas burdened with the knowledge of his instrumental role in the unfolding cosmic drama, continued to play with a mixture of awe and trepidation, aware that his music had become a conduit for eldritch energies that lay dormant in the fabric of reality. The frostbitten transformation carried on, guided by the unseen hands of cosmic entities, as the village square resonated with the cosmic tones of the Yuletide carolers.

As Clara Whitman led the carolers through the snow-kissed village square, her voice resonating with festive cheer, she became an unwitting focal point for an unseen audience. From the shadows, cosmic entities observed the festivities with inscrutable gazes drawn to the harmonious melodies that echoed through the frost-laden air.

Unbeknownst to Clara, her heartfelt singing was a beacon to entities from beyond the veil. These entities had long remained dormant beneath the cosmic currents. As the snowflakes, now imbued with eldritch energies, continued to fall, the watcher in the shadows observed the unfolding events with an intensity that transcended mortal understanding. Clara, the unwitting conduit for cosmic attention, continued her carol with a radiant spirit, unaware of the cosmic forces that now gazed upon the heart of the winter celebration.

As Clara's voice echoed through the village square, an unseen transformation began to weave through the festive scene. Threads of cosmic influence, imperceptible to the revelers, subtly unraveled the joyful celebration into an unknowable cosmic spectacle. The snowflakes, now charged with eldritch energies, danced in intricate patterns, forming ethereal connections that transcended the boundaries of the mundane.

The villagers, caught in the moment's beauty, felt an unspoken shift in the atmosphere. The air seemed to shimmer with a cosmic resonance as if the boundaries between the ordinary and the extraordinary were blurring. Yet, amidst the enchantment, there lingered a subtle undercurrent of something otherworldly—a presence that defied comprehension.

As the carolers continued their procession, the village square transformed into a convergence point where festive merriment and cosmic forces collided, setting the stage for a series of mysterious events that would unfold in the coming nights. The threads of cosmic influence, woven invisibly through the fabric of the Yuletide celebration, hinted at a tapestry of eldritch wonders waiting to be unveiled.

The frostbitten air held lingering echoes of the unknown, a testament to the cosmic forces that had been unwittingly awakened. As the carolers concluded their festive procession, the village square witnessed a subtle but profound shift in the fabric of reality. Like ripples in an unseen pond, the cosmic repercussions were set in motion, destined to reverberate through the subsequent Yuletide nights.

In the aftermath of the carolers' unknowing encounter with the eldritch, the villagers dispersed, carrying a sense of awe and wonder that transcended the usual joy of the season. Unseen entities observed from the shadows, their inscrutable gaze fixed upon the quaint village and its unwitting inhabitants. The stage was now set for a succession of mysterious tales, each destined to unfold under the cosmic influence of the twelve nights of Eldritch Yule.

The Unseen Gift

The festive scene unfolded with familial joy in the Jenkins Residence's heart. The crackling fireplace cast dancing shadows on the walls adorned with traditional Christmas decorations—a tapestry of memories collected over the years. The evergreen scent permeated the air, mingling with the warmth of laughter and the clinking of festive ornaments.

Timothy and Margaret Jenkins moved about with an easy familiarity, their movements synchronized in the festive dance of holiday preparations. The cozy ambiance was a haven of comfort. This haven seemingly shielded them from the mysteries that lingered just beyond the threshold of their domestic bliss.

Adjacent to this idyllic scene, Old Man Barnaby's abode loomed, a shadowy presence in the tranquil neighborhood. The mysterious neighbor's house stood as a silent sentinel, its exterior veiled in an air of enigma. Rumors whispered among the townsfolk and spoke of peculiar occurrences surrounding Barnaby, adding an extra layer of intrigue to his reclusive nature.

As the Jenkins family prepared for the festivities, a subtle shift in the air hinted at the unseen gift that lay in wait. With its cryptic allure, old Man Barnaby's dwelling stood as a gateway to the unknown—a portal through which cosmic wonders would soon spill into the seemingly ordinary setting. The stage was set for a Yuletide night where the line between the mundane and the cosmic would blur, and the true nature of the unseen gift would be revealed in all its eldritch glory.

In the heart of the Jenkins Residence, Timothy, a kind-hearted patriarch, moved with purpose amid the festive preparations. His eyes gleamed with the anticipation of sharing the joyous Yuletide moments with his beloved wife, Margaret. She, in turn, radiated warmth and sincerity, her spirit embracing the essence of Christmas and family.

As the Jenkins family bustled about their cozy abode, the unseen gift lingered in the air—a gift that would soon weave its cosmic threads into the fabric of their celebrations. Meanwhile, just beyond the threshold of their festive haven, Old Man Barnaby observed, his enigmatic presence shrouded in the mystique that whispered of untold secrets.

Old Man Barnaby's reclusive nature had long fueled speculation among the townsfolk. Yet, his connection to a gift that transcended the ordinary remained an enduring mystery. Unaware of the cosmic forces at play, the Jenkins family continued their preparations, unknowingly on the brink of an encounter with the unknown.

As the festive scene unfolded within the Jenkins Residence and Old Man Barnaby's abode, a cosmic tension simmered beneath the surface, promising a Yuletide night where the ordinary would yield to the extraordinary. The stage was set for the revelation of the unseen gift and the cosmic wonders it carried within its mysterious embrace.

Amidst the glow of hearth and home, the Jenkins Residence bathed in the serene ambiance of Christmas Eve. The crackling fireplace cast dancing shadows across the walls adorned with festive decorations, each bauble and strand of tinsel reflecting the warm glow of the season. The air was infused with the comforting scents of pine and cinnamon and the promise of shared laughter and cherished moments.

Timothy and Margaret, the heart of the Jenkins family, moved about the cozy abode with a harmonious rhythm. Their love for each other and the festive spirit echoed in the flicker of candlelight and the joyous sounds emanating from the heart of their home. The aroma of holiday delights wafted from the kitchen, teasing the senses and adding to the anticipation in the air.

The unseen gift lingered in this haven of familial joy, a subtle undercurrent beneath the surface of the Christmas Eve serenity. As the Jenkins family reveled in the moments leading up to the midnight celebration, they remained oblivious to the cosmic forces poised to unfold within the walls of their home.

Outside, Old Man Barnaby's abode stood in mysterious contrast—a silhouette against the frost-kissed night. Within its shadowy confines, the enigmatic neighbor prepared to impart a gift that transcended the ordinary, its cosmic origins echoing in the quietude of the Yuletide night.

The stage was set for a Christmas Eve, where the serenity of familial joy would intertwine with the cosmic mysteries awaiting revelation. As the clock ticked toward midnight, the tapestry of the night held the promise of wonders that transcended the boundaries of tradition and ventured into the realm of the unknown.

Amidst the unassuming evening, Timothy Jenkins, the household patriarch, was drawn to the doorstep by a curiosity that fluttered in the frosty air. The laughter and warmth of familial joy filled the Jenkins Residence. Still, the cosmic allure of the peculiar gift beckoned to Timothy.

As he approached the door, he noticed an intricately wrapped box resting on the threshold, adorned with cryptic symbols that seemed to dance in the flickering glow of the porch light. The cosmic motifs etched onto the wrapping paper hinted at a significance beyond the ordinary, an invitation to unravel mysteries hidden within the folds of the festive tradition.

Timothy's fingers traced the celestial patterns, and with each touch, he felt a subtle vibration, as if the gift itself pulsed with otherworldly energy. The enigma of the moment hung in the frosty air, and the serenity of the Christmas Eve evening became tinged with the anticipation of the unknown.

Unbeknownst to Timothy, the cosmic forces that had been dormant were now awakening, their presence woven into the fabric of the unassuming evening. The veil between the mundane and the eldritch began to thin, and the Jenkins family stood at the threshold of a cosmic revelation that would transcend the boundaries of their familiar Christmas celebration.

As Timothy gingerly unwrapped the enigmatic gift, the room seemed to hold its breath, embracing a moment pregnant with cosmic possibilities. The paper gave way to reveal an otherworldly artifact—a delicate orb bathed in a soft, ethereal glow that transcended the bounds of earthly gifts.

The glow illuminated the room, casting intricate light patterns across the walls. The artifact pulsed with a rhythmic energy as if resonating with the cosmic forces that lingered unseen. Its surface, adorned with symbols reminiscent of ancient constellations, seemed to whisper celestial secrets to those who dared to listen.

In the quiet of the Jenkins Residence, the family gathered around, their expressions a mixture of awe and wonder. With her warm and sincere demeanor, Margaret held her breath, captivated by the unfolding mystery. The artifact, once confined to the confines of wrapping paper, could now transport the Jenkins family beyond ordinary Christmas celebrations.

As the glow expanded, casting its celestial radiance throughout the room, the serenity of the Christmas Eve evening merged with the cosmic energy emanating from the artifact. Unbeknownst to the Jenkins family, their humble abode had become a nexus where the mundane and the eldritch entwined—a place where the veil between worlds began to shimmer with the promise of revelations that transcended the boundaries of Yuletide tradition.

Though usually the embodiment of warmth and sincerity, Margaret couldn't suppress a flicker of skepticism as she gazed upon the unearthly artifact. Her brow furrowed with wonder and concern, creating a tension that echoed through the room. The glow from the cosmic gift danced in her eyes, casting shadows of doubt that mingled with the soft radiance.

Timothy, the kind-hearted patriarch, tried to calm the uncertainty with a reassuring smile, his eyes reflecting a quiet determination to embrace the extraordinary. The children caught between the skepticism of their mother and the wonder sparked by the cosmic glow, exchanged glances that mirrored the cosmic dance of uncertainty and curiosity.

The artifact, now the room's focal point, stood as a symbol of the unseen forces that had chosen this humble abode for a mysterious intersection of worlds. The serenity of the Christmas Eve evening hung in the balance, teetering between the familiar warmth of family tradition and the cosmic unknown that beckoned from within the enigmatic glow.

As the cosmic energies continued to ripple through the room, Margaret's skepticism began to yield to the undeniable allure of the otherworldly gift. Once clouded with doubt, her eyes now sparkled with a curiosity that mirrored the cosmic mysteries hidden within the artifact. The stage was set for a familial journey that would transcend the ordinary boundaries of Christmas Eve, plunging the Jenkins family into a cosmic adventure that defied the constraints of the expected.

Old Man Barnaby stepped onto the Jenkins family porch with a presence that seemed to materialize from the shadows themselves. His figure, draped in the mystery of the night, cast an enigmatic silhouette against the glow of the cosmic artifact. The Jenkins family, caught in a moment suspended between skepticism and wonder, watched as he approached with measured steps as though guided by the unseen forces wading through the frosty air.

With a knowing glint in his eyes, Barnaby began to unravel the cosmic tapestry surrounding the unearthly gift. He spoke cryptically, his words carrying the weight of ancient wisdom and cosmic revelations. As he wove a narrative that intertwined the earthly traditions of Christmas with the cosmic energies that pulsed within the artifact, the Jenkins family found themselves drawn into a surreal revelation that transcended the boundaries of their cozy Christmas Eve.

The reclusive neighbor's visit became a journey into the cosmic unknown, a guided tour through realms where the mundane and the eldritch converged. The glow from the artifact seemed to respond to Barnaby's words, flickering in rhythmic harmony with the cosmic truths he unveiled. Skepticism gave way to fascination, and wonder blossomed in the eyes of the Jenkins family, now participants in a Yuletide tale that defied the ordinary and embraced the cosmic wonders that lurked beneath the surface of their cozy Christmas Eve.

The Jenkins living room, once a haven of familial warmth, underwent a metamorphosis beneath the influence of the unearthly artifact. As Old Man Barnaby continued to unravel the cosmic secrets, an ethereal glow enveloped the room, painting the walls with hues unseen in the spectrum of earthly colors. The air shimmered with an energy transcending the mundane, and the boundaries between the familiar and the cosmic began to blur.

The ordinary furniture and decorations took on an otherworldly sheen, and the cosmic threshold manifested in the very fabric of the room. Like the resonance of distant stars, a subtle hum filled the air, creating an ambiance that defied the constraints of earthly existence. The Jenkins family stood on the brink of an extraordinary revelation, their living room now a portal to realms beyond the veil of reality.

Once dormant in the artifact, the cosmic energies now surged and pulsed, creating a tangible connection between the Jenkins residence and the unseen dimensions that lay just beyond their perception. The threshold beckoned, inviting them to enter the unknown and embrace the cosmic mysteries that awaited on the other side. This Yuletide journey promised to unfold across twelve nights of eldritch wonder.

Timothy and Margaret stood at the precipice of a decision that would shape the course of their Christmas Eve. The cosmic threshold, aglow with unearthly radiance, presented them with a choice that resonated with wonder and trepidation. As the ethereal hum filled the room, Old Man Barnaby, the harbinger of cosmic revelations, observed their contemplation with an inscrutable gaze.

Margaret's eyes flickered between skepticism and wonder, caught in the tension between the known's safety and the cosmic unknown's allure. The cosmic energies pulsed, inviting them to transcend the boundaries of the ordinary and embrace the eldritch mysteries woven into the fabric of the artifact.

Old Man Barnaby, with a demeanor that hinted at the weight of cosmic wisdom, spoke cryptically of the potential consequences and the cosmic dance awaiting those who dared to take the step. The choice was between staying and going and between the comfort of the familiar and the cosmic adventure that beckoned beyond the threshold.

The Jenkins family stood at the crossroads of reality and cosmic wonder, their decision echoing through the frostbitten air, intertwining with the unseen forces that awaited the unraveling of Yuletide mysteries. The cosmic revelation teased, promising an intricate dance of joy and dread to unfold across the twelve nights of Eldritch Yule.

The threshold embraced the Jenkins family, enveloping them in a surreal cascade of cosmic energies. As they emerged on the other side, the ordinary living room transformed into a gateway to unseen realms, where the laws of reality yielded to the whims of eldritch forces.

The landscape unfolded before them, a tapestry of cosmic vistas that defied earthly comprehension. Nebulas of vibrant hues painted the sky, celestial bodies pulsed with ethereal light, and surreal dimensions intertwined in a dance of cosmic majesty. It was a realm where the mundane and the eldritch coexisted in a harmonious, albeit enigmatic, ballet.

Beyond the scope of mortal understanding, Eldritch entities moved through the astral planes with otherworldly grace. Their forms flickered with cosmic energy, whispering secrets that transcended language. The Jenkins family, once tethered to the earthly plane, now found themselves adrift in a cosmic sea of wonders.

Amidst the awe-inspiring spectacle, the family grappled with the revelation of unseen realms and the cosmic mysteries that beckoned. The choice made in the cozy living room resonated through the cosmic tapestry, weaving their destinies into the eldritch dance that would unfold across the twelve nights of Eldritch Yule.

As swiftly as it had opened, the cosmic portal closed, leaving the Jenkins family on the brink of the unknown. Once a cosmic threshold, the living room returned to its familiar state, the warmth of Christmas lights replacing the surreal vistas of cosmic realms.

The Jenkins family, their senses still tingling with the lingering energies of the eldritch journey, stared at the ordinary room now infused with the memory of the cosmic tapestry they had briefly traversed. The veil between the mundane and the cosmic had reasserted itself, concealing the mysteries that awaited them in the subsequent Yuletide nights.

Uncertainty hung in the air, a palpable tension between the known's safety and the unknown's allure. The cosmic energies, having woven their influence into the fabric of the Jenkins family's reality, left an indelible mark on their souls. As Christmas Eve waned into the night, the anticipation of what lay beyond the veil lingered—a cosmic enigma that would unfold in the twelve nights of Eldritch Yule.

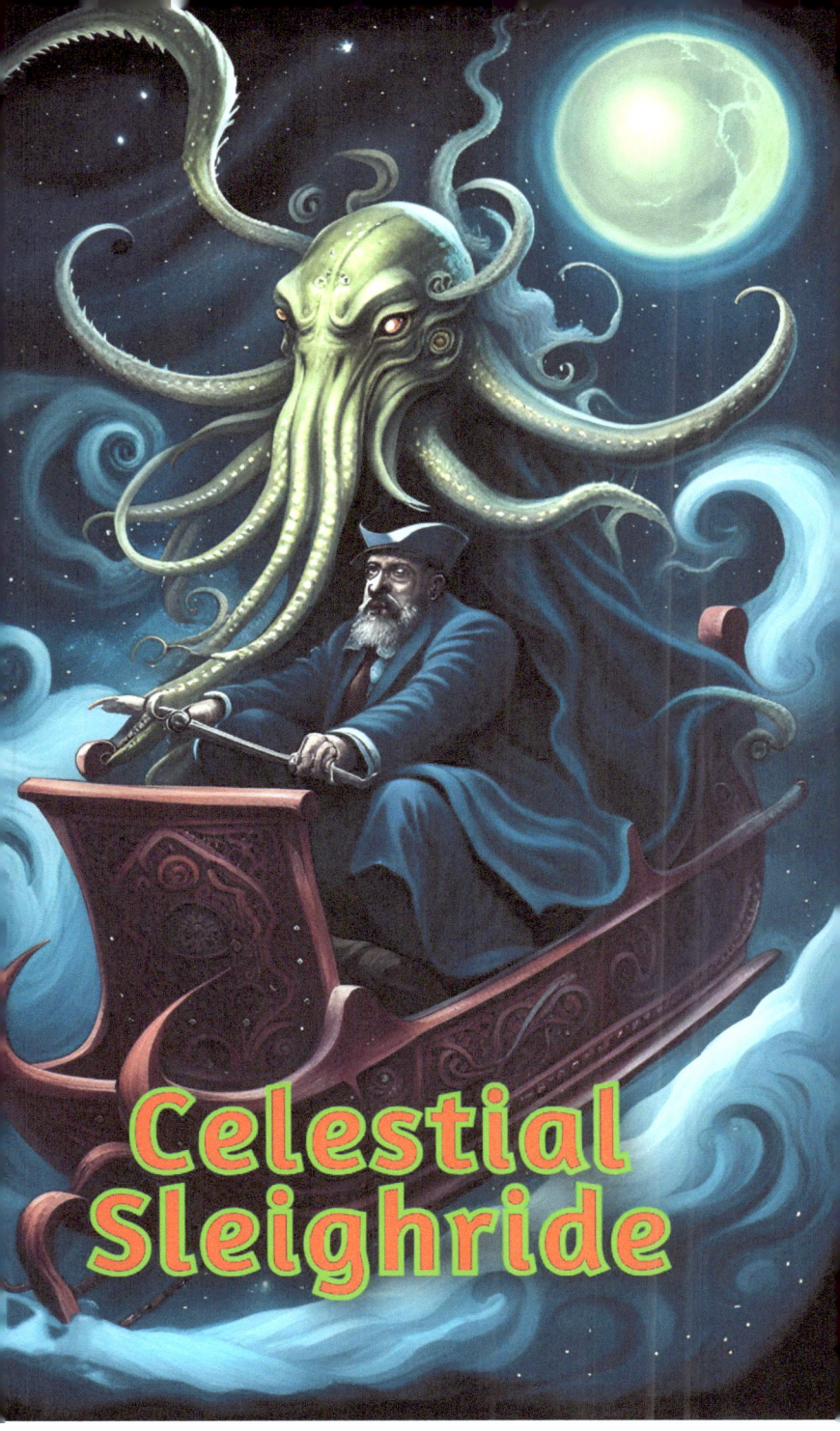

Celestial Sleighride

Amidst the Thompson Residence, a haven of familial warmth, the hearth fires cast a flickering glow against walls adorned with festive decorations. Laughter and joy reverberated through the air, intertwining with the crackle of the fire, creating a cocoon of comfort that shielded the family from the winter's chill. Unbeknownst to them, a cosmic spectacle was about to unfold within the cozy embrace of their home.

The living room, aglow with the festive spirit, was the nucleus for the Thompson family's holiday gathering. The celestial ballet began to unfurl above as generations came together, exchanging tales and sharing the season's spirit. High in the cosmic expanse, a celestial sleigh embarked on a route that transcended the familiar constellations, leaving trails of cosmic dust that sparkled like distant stars.

The celestial sleigh itself, adorned with ethereal lights that mirrored the brilliance of the heavens, moved with a grace that seemed to defy the laws of earthly physics. Its journey is carved through the cosmic tapestry, a mesmerizing dance of celestial wonders. Yet, below in the Thompson Residence, the family remained blissfully unaware of the cosmic drama unfolding above.

As the sleigh traversed its celestial route, the earthly home below continued to bask in the warm glow of Christmas lights. Though unseen by the Thompsons, each twinkle in the sky was a beacon of cosmic energies weaving a story that surpassed the boundaries of the mundane. The celestial sleigh ride became a bridge between the ordinary and the cosmic, a phenomenon hidden from earthly eyes but hinting at the extraordinary revelations awaiting discovery in the enchanting Yuletide nights ahead.

Amelia Thompson, with eyes full of wonder and a heart brimming with imagination, found herself drawn to the ethereal glow of the celestial sleigh that danced across the cosmic canvas. Amid the Thompson Residence's festive cheer, she sensed a cosmic calling, an invitation to embark on a journey that transcended the ordinary boundaries of the Yuletide season.

Amelia's breath caught in the wintry air as she gazed through the frost-kissed window. The celestial sleigh, adorned with lights mirrored the brilliance of distant galaxies, seemed to beckon her into the realms beyond. It was a siren call to a cosmic adventure waiting to unfold, and the spirited protagonist felt an irresistible pull to become part of the celestial ballet.

Amelia's eyes widened with awe as the celestial pilot, an enigmatic figure draped in cosmic attire, emerged in her imagination. The pilot embodied the essence of Yuletide magic, a being woven from the fabric of eldritch mysteries and festive enchantment. With a cosmic wink and a gesture that spoke the language of the stars, the celestial pilot invited Amelia to join the celestial sleigh ride and explore the cosmic wonders that awaited.

In the cozy haven of the Thompson Residence, the ordinary transformed into the extraordinary. As the celestial sleigh continued its celestial route, Amelia stood at the threshold of a cosmic journey, her heart beating in harmony with the celestial energies. The air shimmered with the promise of cosmic revelations, and the celestial pilot guided her, ready to unveil the secrets of the Yuletide nights that lay beyond the veil of the familiar. The stage was set for an adventure transcending the boundaries of imagination, inviting Amelia to embrace the cosmic mysteries that awaited her in the celestial sleigh ride of Eldritch Yule.

In the heart of the Thompson Residence, Christmas Eve unfolded in an atmosphere of tranquility and familial warmth. The crackling hearth cast a gentle glow across the room, its flickering flames dancing harmoniously with the festive decorations adorning the walls. The scent of evergreen and the soft melody of classic carols filled the air, wrapping the home in a cocoon of timeless holiday magic.

Amelia's family moved with purpose, each member contributing to preparing a traditional Christmas celebration. The sound of laughter and the clinking of ornaments created a symphony of joy, echoing through the cozy rooms. As the family gathered around the fireplace, sharing stories and sipping on cups of hot cocoa, the simple pleasure of togetherness became the heartwarming centerpiece of the evening.

Outside, snowflakes gently descended from the heavens, adding a touch of magic to the wintry scene. The Thompson Residence, adorned with twinkling lights and wreaths, stood as a haven of serenity amidst the hushed landscape. Though a distant dream in the cosmic tapestry, the celestial sleigh was momentarily forgotten as the family reveled in the beauty of the present moment.

The Christmas tree, adorned with heirloom ornaments and memories of years gone by, stood tall in the corner, a testament to the enduring spirit of the season. In this moment of tranquility, the cosmic wonders and eldritch mysteries took a backseat to the simple joys of family, tradition, and the magic that lingered on this enchanting Christmas Eve.

As the night deepened, the Thompson family, wrapped in the warmth of familial bonds, looked forward to the celestial sleigh ride that awaited them, unaware of the cosmic wonders that would unfold in the subsequent Yuletide nights. The stage was set for a harmonious blend of earthly traditions and cosmic enchantment in the quietude of the Thompson Residence on this magical Christmas Eve.

Amelia's childhood wonder, ignited by the timeless tales of celestial sleighs and cosmic wonders passed down through generations, was the spark to set the stage for extraordinary events on this magical Christmas Eve. The young protagonist, with eyes aglow and a heart brimming with anticipation, was caught in the delicate dance between the enchanting stories of old and the cosmic mysteries that beckoned from beyond.

As the Thompson family continued their preparations, Amelia's gaze often wandered beyond the cozy confines of the home, drawn to the starlit sky where dreams and reality blurred into one. The celestial sleigh, a mere figment of folklore, became a beacon of possibility, its existence hanging in the delicate balance between imagination and the uncharted realms of the cosmos.

In the quiet moments when the festivities paused, Amelia daydreamed about the celestial pilot—whose cosmic attire and otherworldly aura transcended the boundaries of earthly folklore. The stories had spoken of a magical being draped in the brilliance of Yuletide magic, guiding a celestial sleigh through the celestial tapestry. On this fateful night, the boundaries between fantasy and reality began to waver, and the cosmic wonders teased the edge of the tangible.

The celestial sleigh, wrapped in the ethereal glow of starlight, made its silent approach to the Thompson Residence. It traversed the cosmic tapestry unseen by earthly eyes, responding to the whispers of childhood wonder that lingered in the frosty air. Amelia's imagination had unwittingly summoned the cosmic pilot, setting in motion a journey that would transcend the boundaries of ordinary Christmas celebrations.

As the clock ticked toward midnight, the celestial sleigh hovered just beyond the veil of perception, waiting for the moment when childhood wonder would bridge the gap between the mundane and the cosmic. The stage was set for a celestial sleigh ride that would transport Amelia and her family into realms where the wonders of imagination intertwined with the cosmic mysteries hidden in the depths of the winter night.

The celestial sleigh made its otherworldly arrival, descending from the cosmic heights with a grace that defied earthly physics. Its descent was a silent ballet of celestial proportions, drawing the gaze of the Thompson family and, beyond, the entire neighborhood.

As the sleigh touched down on the snow-covered lawn of the Thompson Residence, it created a luminous imprint. This otherworldly landing left the air tingling with cosmic energies. The ethereal glow from the sleigh bathed the surroundings in a celestial luminescence, casting long shadows that danced in harmony with the cosmic mysteries at play.

The neighborhood, wrapped in the hush of the winter night, witnessed a spectacle beyond their wildest imaginations. Windows lit up as curious onlookers peered out, drawn by an invisible force to witness the celestial sleigh ride that had materialized on this enchanted Christmas Eve.

Standing at the forefront of the spectacle, Amelia felt the pull of the cosmic energies. Her childhood wonder had unfurled a cosmic tapestry. Now, in the glow of the celestial arrival, she was poised on the threshold between the familiar and the unknown.

The celestial pilot stepped gracefully from the sleigh, draped in cosmic attire that shimmered like the constellations themselves. Their presence carried the weight of Yuletide's magic and eldritch mysteries. This being embodied the very essence of the cosmic forces that had been awakened.

Amelia's family and the gathered neighbors stood in awe as the celestial pilot extended a hand—an invitation to embark on a sleigh ride that would transcend the boundaries of the ordinary. The neighborhood, once bound by the constraints of reality, now found itself on the cusp of a cosmic journey, where the wonders of the universe awaited those who dared to believe.

And so, with the celestial sleigh awaiting its passengers, the Thompson family and their neighbors faced a choice. This choice would lead them into the depths of the cosmic unknown, where the celestial sleigh ride promised to unveil the mysteries that lay beyond the veil of the starlit sky.

Amelia, compelled by an irresistible force that seemed to emanate from the celestial sleigh, stepped outside into the frosty night. Her breath hung in the air as she gazed upward, her eyes fixed on the ethereal spectacle that hovered above—the celestial sleigh adorned in cosmic splendor, shimmering with eldritch energies that defied the laws of the mundane.

The celestial pilot, draped in cosmic attire, acknowledged Amelia's presence with a nod. In that silent gesture, an unspoken connection formed—an understanding transcending earthly comprehension's boundaries. It was as if the cosmos had chosen Amelia, drawing her into the cosmic dance that unfolded on this extraordinary Christmas Eve.

The neighborhood, bathed in the celestial glow, watched as Amelia approached the sleigh with a mixture of trepidation and fascination. The air crackled with otherworldly energy, and the ordinary confines of reality seemed to blur as Amelia took her place beside the celestial pilot.

As the celestial sleigh prepared to embark on its cosmic journey, the onlookers felt a subtle shift in the atmosphere. The celestial energies woven into the night fabric created a palpable anticipation. This cosmic resonance echoed through the stillness of the winter air.

With a graceful motion, the celestial pilot signaled, and the sleigh rose gently into the cosmic expanse, leaving behind the familiar landscape of the Thompson Residence and venturing into the realms beyond the earthly horizon. Amelia, with wide eyes filled with wonder, became a participant in a Yuletide adventure that transcended the boundaries of reality, carried aloft by the celestial sleigh on a journey through the cosmic mysteries that awaited in the frost-kissed night.

Standing beneath the celestial sleigh's ethereal glow, Amelia found herself in an otherworldly encounter with the celestial pilot—an enigmatic figure draped in cosmic attire. The air around them vibrated with subtle energy as if the very fabric of reality yielded to the cosmic forces at play.

The celestial pilot, with eyes that held the mysteries of the cosmos, extended an invitation to Amelia. It wasn't spoken in words but communicated through a profound connection that transcended the limits of ordinary human understanding. In that silent exchange, a cosmic pact was forged, and the boundaries of reality began to blur.

Amelia, captivated by the celestial pilot's gaze and the allure of the sleigh, felt an irresistible pull. Without hesitation, she accepted the cosmic invitation, stepping into the sleigh with wonder and trepidation. The transition was seamless, as if the sleigh existed in the space between worlds, bridging the mundane and the cosmic.

As the celestial sleigh ascended into the star-strewn sky, leaving the familiar surroundings of her home behind, Amelia marveled at the cosmic vistas that unfolded before her. The celestial pilot guided the sleigh through realms where the ordinary laws of nature gave way to the extraordinary, and the boundaries of the known universe became fluid.

Amelia, now a passenger on this celestial sleigh ride, embraced the cosmic adventure that awaited her—a journey through the tapestry of the cosmos, where each twinkling star held a story, and the cosmic energies resonated with the spirit of Yuletide magic. Together with the celestial pilot, she soared through the cosmic expanse, leaving behind the earthly realm for a celestial odyssey that promised revelations beyond the grasp of mortal understanding.

As the celestial sleigh traversed the cosmic tapestry, Amelia marveled at the celestial route that unfolded before her. Beyond the stars, the astral journey led through realms that defied earthly comprehension. Each twist and turn of the celestial path revealed celestial wonders, eldritch landscapes, and cosmic phenomena that danced in harmony with the spirit of Yuletide magic.

The celestial pilot guided the sleigh with a cosmic grace, navigating through constellations that pulsed with ethereal energies. Sitting beside the enigmatic figure, Amelia felt the resonance of cosmic forces that permeated the very essence of the celestial route. It was a journey beyond the mundane, where the laws of physics yielded to the whims of the cosmic unknown.

As they soared through the vastness of space, Amelia glimpsed celestial entities—living constellations that shimmered with eldritch radiance. These cosmic beings, guardians of the astral realms, observed the sleigh's passage with inscrutable gazes, their forms shifting and merging in patterns that echoed the mysteries of the cosmos.

The celestial route took them through nebulous clouds that sparkled with the dust of distant galaxies and ethereal landscapes where time seemed to warp and twist. Each moment of the journey unfolded like a page in a cosmic time, revealing the interconnectedness of the universe and the eldritch forces that lay hidden behind the veil of reality.

As the celestial sleigh ride continued, the celestial pilot and Amelia ventured deeper into the cosmic unknown, leaving behind the familiar constellations of the night sky. The astral journey promised celestial wonders and the unveiling of cosmic secrets that transcended the boundaries of mortal understanding. Like a celestial symphony, the celestial route played on, resonating with the celestial energies that echoed through the Yuletide night.

Amelia listened intently as the celestial sleigh soared through the cosmos, the ethereal winds carrying whispers of cosmic secrets. The celestial pilot, draped in cosmic attire, began to unveil revelations that transcended the ordinary understanding of Christmas magic.

The enigmatic figure spoke of ancient cosmic pacts forged in the distant reaches of the universe, where eldritch forces and the spirit of Christmas intertwined in a dance of cosmic harmony. Whispers of celestial beings older than time echoed through the astral expanse, sharing tales of Yuletide celebrations in realms beyond mortal perception.

As the celestial sleigh ride continued, the celestial pilot wove a cosmic narrative that connected the festive joy of Christmas with the cosmic energies that pulsed through the universe. The celestial secrets revealed the role of Yuletide in maintaining the delicate balance between cosmic forces, a balance upheld by the collective merriment and goodwill of those who celebrated the season.

Amelia marveled at the intricate dance of cosmic energies, the unseen threads that bound the magic of Christmas to the cosmic tapestry. The revelations unfolded like constellations in the night sky, each adding a new layer to the cosmic tale that played out against the backdrop of the Yuletide night.

The celestial pilot's words resonated with a celestial melody, merging the enchantment of Christmas with the eldritch mysteries that lay hidden in the depths of the cosmos. As the celestial sleigh glided through the astral realms, the whispers of cosmic secrets became a symphony of knowledge, enriching the ride with a profound understanding of the cosmic forces that shaped the Yuletide magic.

As the celestial sleigh continued its astral journey through the cosmic realms, Amelia found herself in the company of unseen companions—ethereal entities and celestial beings that emerged from the fabric of the universe itself. Each encounter added a new layer to the unfolding cosmic tapestry, expanding the scope of Yuletide magic and eldritch wonders.

Among the celestial entities were luminous beings of pure energy, their presence radiating warmth and benevolence. They whispered tales of ancient celebrations in distant galaxies, where the magic of Christmas intertwined with cosmic energies to create breathtaking celestial displays.

Amelia marveled at the diversity of her unseen companions. Some resembled celestial musicians, playing ethereal melodies that resonated with the cosmic vibrations of the universe. Others took on forms reminiscent of celestial dancers, gracefully twirling amidst the astral expanse, their movements synchronized with the rhythm of cosmic forces.

Amelia engaged in silent conversations with these cosmic entities as the celestial sleigh ride continued. They shared cosmic wisdom, revealing the intricate connections between the magic of Christmas and the cosmic energies that permeated every corner of the universe. Each entity contributed a unique perspective, painting a vivid portrait of the cosmic celebration that transcended mortal understanding.

The astral journey became a dance of communion between Amelia and the unseen companions, a harmonious exchange of energies transcending the ordinary's boundaries. Together, they traversed through celestial landscapes adorned with cosmic wonders, each encounter leaving an indelible mark on the cosmic tapestry woven across the Yuletide night.

As the celestial sleigh continued its celestial route, the unseen companions guided Amelia through the cosmic mysteries, unraveling the threads that connected Christmas's festive spirit with the cosmos' vastness. The celestial tapestry expanded with each passing moment, revealing a cosmic celebration that echoed across the celestial realms, an everlasting symphony of Yuletide magic and eldritch wonders.

In the cosmic expanse of the celestial sleigh ride, Amelia found herself entwined in a temporal conundrum—a paradoxical dance through moments that seemed to stretch into infinity. The astral journey unfolded in a way that defied the conventional flow of earthly time, transcending the limitations of past, present, and future.

As the sleigh traversed celestial realms, each moment became an eternal now, a suspended instance in the cosmic tapestry where the boundaries of time blurred into a seamless continuum. The stars seemed to pulse with the universe's heartbeat, synchronizing with the rhythm of Yuletide magic that resonated through the cosmic expanse.

C caught in the temporal conundrum, Amelia experienced a cascade of cosmic sensations. The celestial sleigh ride became a journey through the very fabric of time, where the past, present, and future coexisted in a harmonious dance. The ethereal entities accompanying her whispered tales of ancient celebrations and future festivities, weaving a narrative transcending earthly time's linear progression.

The astral landscapes they traversed were not bound by the ticking of clocks or the turning of calendars. Instead, each moment unfolded as a cosmic event, an eternal celebration that echoed across the celestial realms. The ephemeral nature of the celestial sleigh ride became a testament to the timelessness of Yuletide magic. In this experience, the concept of past and future merged into an everlasting present.

As Amelia gazed upon the cosmic wonders that unfolded around her, she embraced the temporal conundrum with a sense of wonder and acceptance. The celestial sleigh ride became a journey through the tapestry of time, a kaleidoscopic exploration of moments beyond earthly understanding.

In this cosmic dance of temporal mysteries, Amelia discovered that the ephemeral nature of the celestial sleigh ride held the key to unlocking the secrets of Yuletide magic. This timeless celebration echoed through the cosmic tapestry, leaving an indelible mark on the fabric of the universe itself.

The ethereal journey through cosmic realms ended as the celestial sleigh gracefully descended, returning to the familiar surroundings of the Thompson Residence. Amelia, with a heart brimming with cosmic wonders, stepped out of the astral vehicle and onto the earthly grounds, feeling the transition from celestial splendor to the cozy ambiance of her home.

The celestial pilot, draped in cosmic attire, bid her farewell with a nod, acknowledging the unspoken connection forged through the journey. As the celestial sleigh departed into the night sky, leaving behind a trail of shimmering stardust, Amelia couldn't shake the sense of having glimpsed a reality beyond reality. In this realm, Yuletide's magic and cosmic mysteries converged.

Unaware of the cosmic odyssey that had unfolded, the Thompson family continued their Christmas Eve celebration inside. The cozy home environment, aglow with hearth fires and adorned with festive decorations, welcomed Amelia back into the fold of familial joy and traditional merriment.

Yet, in the quiet moments of the night, as she nestled into the familiar surroundings, Amelia carried with her the echoes of the celestial sleigh ride. The return to reality marked not only the end of a cosmic journey but the beginning of a new understanding that transcended earthly celebrations' boundaries.

Having traversed the celestial tapestry, the celestial sleigh left a subtle imprint on the Thompson Residence. The air seemed charged with the lingering magic of the astral voyage as if the very walls held whispers of cosmic secrets. The ornaments and decorations sparkled with an otherworldly glow, a testament to the unseen companions and celestial beings accompanying Amelia on her ethereal adventure.

The celestial sleigh ride became a cherished memory as the night unfolded and Christmas dawned on the horizon. This cosmic gift transcended the material realm. The return to reality did not diminish the magic; instead, it enriched the festive atmosphere with the cosmic energy woven into the fabric of the universe.

With a heart now tuned to the celestial frequencies, Amelia joined her family in the joyous celebration, knowing that the cosmic wonders she had witnessed would forever be a part of the timeless enchantment of Yuletide magic.

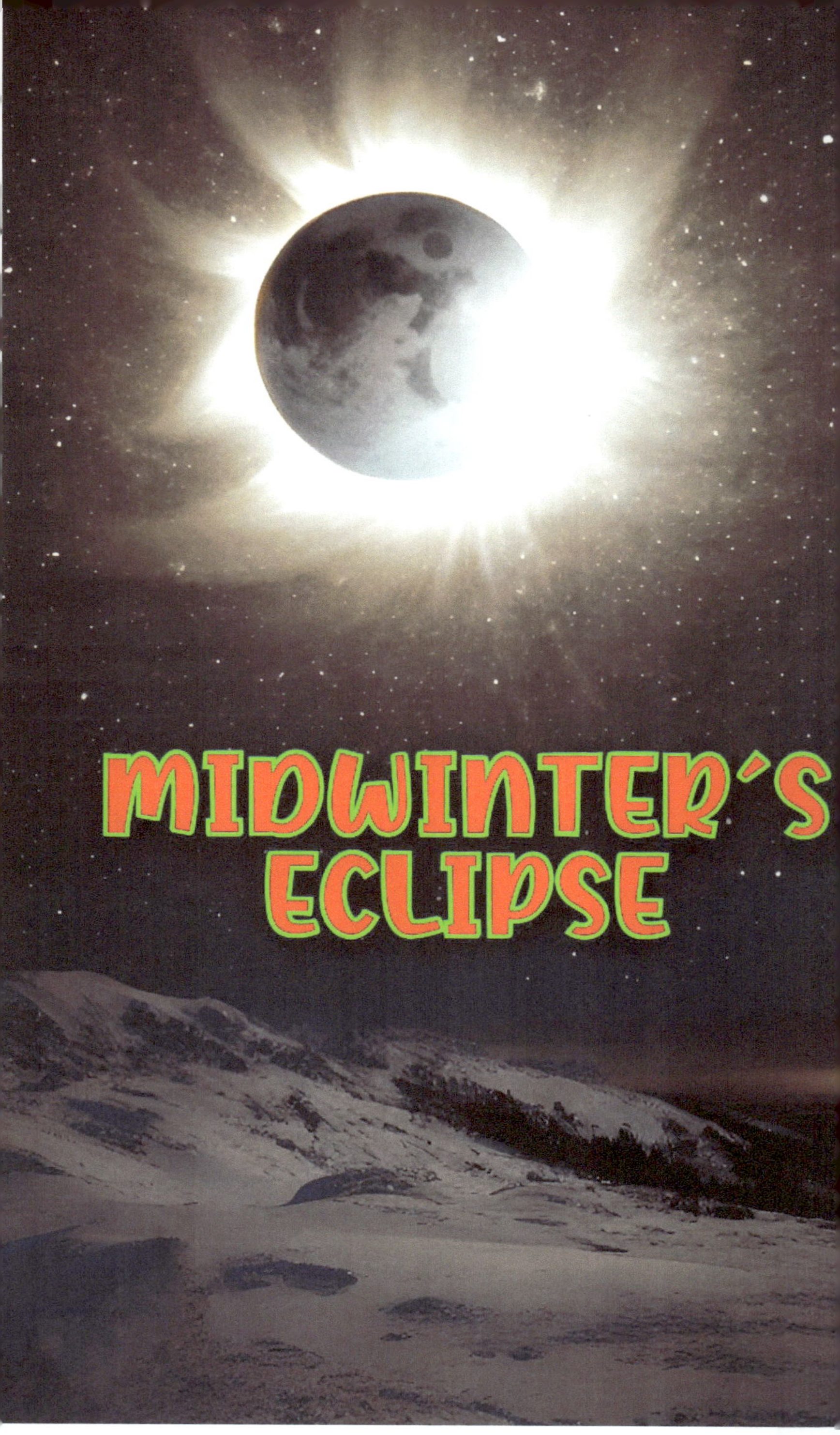
MIDWINTER'S
ECLIPSE

In the heart of the town, where the cosmic dance of stars and the revelry of Midwinter converged, stood the Town Observatory. In this celestial hub, astronomers and mystics gathered to witness the intricate patterns of the night sky. The domed structure, adorned with astronomical instruments and arcane symbols, marked the convergence of earthly and cosmic realms.

As the townsfolk embraced the magic of Midwinter, the Town Center became a bustling nexus of activity. Festive stalls adorned with winter trinkets lined the streets, and the air was filled with the intoxicating aroma of spiced treats. Laughter echoed through the crisp winter night as families reveled in the joyous atmosphere, their breath visible in the frosty air.

Amid this cosmic celebration, the celestial hub and the town's central square became entwined, bridging the gap between the earthly festivities and the celestial wonders overhead. The observatory, perched on a hill, offered an unobstructed view of the cosmos, making it the ideal vantage point for those seeking to witness the celestial spectacle promised by Midwinter's Eclipse.

Astronomers and curious onlookers gathered at the observatory, their gazes fixed on the above celestial canvas. The winter solstice had arrived, with it, the promise of a rare cosmic event. This eclipse would cast a celestial glow over the town, blending the mundane with the extraordinary.

Meanwhile, the Town Center pulsed with the vibrancy of Midwinter's festivities. Street performers entertained the crowds with enchanting displays while the aroma of mulled cider and roasted chestnuts filled the air. Though distinct in purpose, the celestial hub and the town square shared a cosmic connection that amplified the magic of the winter solstice.

As the night unfolded and the eclipse began to cast its ethereal glow, the boundary between the observable and the unseen blurred. The townsfolk, whether gazing through telescopes at the observatory or reveling in the festivities below, became part of a larger cosmic narrative—a tapestry woven with threads of earthly joy and celestial wonders.

The Midwinter's Eclipse, a celestial ballet between the moon and the sun, painted the town in hues of cosmic radiance. It was a moment where the cosmic energies, stirred by the celestial alignment, interacted with the festivities below, creating an atmosphere tinged with magic and mystery.

Amidst the celestial hubbub, the town's inhabitants found themselves drawn into a cosmic dance, their spirits lifted by the convergence of Midwinter's magic and the cosmic forces that illuminated the night sky. As the eclipse reached its zenith, the observatory and the Town Center became focal points for a celestial communion that transcended earthly celebration boundaries and ventured into the realms of cosmic awe.

Dr. Victoria Monroe, an eminent astronomer passionate about peering into the celestial unknown, stood within the hallowed halls of the Town Observatory. Her eyes, accustomed to scanning the vast tapestry of stars, were alight with anticipation as she prepared for the rare celestial event—the Midwinter's Eclipse. Surrounded by the intricate instruments of her trade, she felt a palpable connection to the cosmic forces that pulsed through the observatory.

On the other side of the cosmic spectrum stood James Reed, a charismatic figure known for his fervent celebration of the winter solstice. Unbeknownst to him, his exuberance and infectious joy resonated with the unseen energies that swirled around the Town Center. As he reveled in the festivities, the cosmic threads subtly wove themselves into the fabric of his merriment.

As the celestial drama unfolded, Dr. Monroe peered through the observatory's telescope, her keen eyes capturing the nuances of the eclipse. The cosmic ballet of the moon and sun, amplified by the alignment of stars, painted the night sky with hues of cosmic radiance. Victoria, usually grounded in the empirical, couldn't help but feel the stirrings of something extraordinary. This cosmic revelation transcended the boundaries of her scientific understanding.

Down below, James Reed found himself in the heart of the Town Center's jubilant celebration. The Midwinter's Eclipse added an ethereal glow to the festivities, and the air buzzed with a subtle energy. Unseen forces intertwined with the laughter and music, creating an atmosphere of enchantment that James, in his revelry, felt but could not fully comprehend.

The cosmic forces at play became more pronounced as the eclipse reached its zenith. Torn between her scientific discipline and the eldritch wonders unfolding before her, Dr. Victoria Monroe felt the boundary between the observable and the unseen blur. Though physically separate, the celestial hub and the Town Center resonated with the same cosmic frequencies, creating a symphony of energies that echoed through the night.

Amidst the revelry, James Reed became an unwitting conduit for the cosmic forces. His celebratory spirit, touched by the unseen threads, took on an otherworldly quality. The joyous shouts and laughter of the townsfolk, now infused with cosmic resonance, echoed through the cosmos, reaching realms beyond mortal comprehension.

As the Midwinter's Eclipse drew close, Dr. Monroe and James Reed found themselves forever changed by the cosmic communion they had experienced. Though distinct in purpose, the observatory and the Town Center had become intertwined nodes in the cosmic network. In this tapestry, earthly celebration and celestial revelations converged, leaving an indelible mark on the town and its inhabitants.

The Town Observatory, nestled atop a hill and shrouded in the velvety darkness of the winter night, stood as a haven for those enraptured by the mysteries of the cosmos. Like an ancient celestial crown, its domed roof embraced a collection of telescopes poised to pierce the veil of the starry tapestry above. Dr. Victoria Monroe, a stalwart seeker of cosmic truths, found solace within its walls, surrounded by the soft hum of instruments and the gentle glow of star charts.

The observatory's interior exuded an air of quiet reverence as astronomers and enthusiasts gathered to witness the celestial wonders unfurling above. Telescopes, each a portal to distant galaxies and cosmic enigmas, stood sentinel against the inky backdrop of the night. The observers, their eyes aglow with anticipation, moved with measured grace, adjusting lenses and charts to capture fleeting glimpses of astral phenomena.

Victoria Monroe, a dedicated steward of the observatory, stood before a massive telescope, her eyes reflecting the glittering constellations she sought to understand. The Starry Haven, as the observatory was affectionately known, became a conduit for cosmic communion. In this place, earthly souls reached out to touch the celestial mysteries that danced in the night sky.

Outside, the winter night embraced the observatory like a cosmic cloak. Scattered like luminescent gems, the stars held tales of distant worlds and ancient secrets. As the observers gazed upward, the boundary between Earth and the cosmos blurred, and the town below became a mere speck in the grand tapestry of the universe.

The observatory's dome, a celestial window to the infinite, echoed with whispers of cosmic revelations. Standing amidst the instruments of her trade, Victoria Monroe felt the weight of the universe pressing upon her. It was not merely a scientific pursuit but a communion with the sublime, a journey into the cosmic unknown that left an indelible mark on those who dared to gaze beyond.

As the night unfolded, the Town Observatory remained a Starry Haven—a sanctuary where the mysteries of the cosmos were unveiled, and the line between the mundane and the eldritch was blurred by the celestial dance overhead. In the quiet hum of cosmic exploration, the observers found a connection to something vast and timeless, a reminder that even in the stillness of a winter night, the universe whispered its secrets to those willing to listen.

With an unwavering passion for unraveling the celestial mysteries, Dr. Victoria Monroe devoted her life to studying the cosmos. Her days were spent immersed in the intricate dance of planets, the shimmering radiance of distant stars, and the enigmatic allure of cosmic phenomena.

In the heart of the Starry Haven, surrounded by the soft glow of starlight and the hum of astronomical instruments, Dr. Monroe's eyes sparkled with the same celestial curiosity that had fueled her journey into the realm of the unknown. The observatory's walls were adorned with charts mapping the trajectories of celestial bodies, and shelves held volumes thick with the accumulated wisdom of ages devoted to studying the cosmos.

Victoria's fingers moved with a practiced grace as she calibrated telescopes, her mind attuned to the intricate ballet of heavenly bodies. Her passion for astronomy transcended the boundaries of earthly knowledge, reaching into the vast expanse of the universe. It was a quest for understanding, a relentless pursuit of answers to questions whispered by the stars.

As the winter solstice approached, Dr. Monroe's excitement intensified. The cosmic energies that wove through the fabric of reality seemed to resonate with her very being. The observatory became not just a workplace but a sacred space where her passion for astronomy transformed into a communion with the cosmic forces that governed the universe.

In the dim light of the observatory, Victoria's silhouette moved against the starlit backdrop, a testament to her unwavering dedication to exploring the unknown. Her notebooks, filled with meticulous observations and sketches, told a story of a scientist driven by an insatiable curiosity—a seeker of cosmic truths navigating the vast tapestry of the cosmos.

The passion for astronomy that burned within Dr. Victoria Monroe's soul was a beacon, drawing others into the orbit of her cosmic journey. As the winter solstice approached, the celestial dance above mirrored the intricate patterns of her life's work, and the Starry Haven awaited the revelation of cosmic secrets that would unfold with the changing of the celestial guard.

James Reed, a charismatic figure in the town, stood at the forefront of the winter solstice celebrations, orchestrating the revelry with infectious enthusiasm.

With a magnetic personality that drew people in, James was the driving force behind the vibrant festivities that brought the community together during the year's longest night.

The Town Center, adorned with winter decorations and bathed in the soft glow of lanterns, became the epicenter of solstice revelry. James's voice rang out above the joyful chatter, his spirited laughter harmonizing with the festive melodies that filled the crisp winter air. Dressed in festive attire, he embodied the season's spirit, weaving a tapestry of warmth and camaraderie.

Under James's guidance, the townsfolk engaged in many activities, from traditional dances around the solstice bonfire to exchanging handmade gifts that reflected the spirit of community and shared joy. The air was filled with the aroma of winter treats, and children's laughter echoed against the backdrop of celestial wonders.

As the night unfolded, James's magnetic presence seemed to amplify the cosmic energies that permeated the winter solstice. The celestial tapestry above mirrored the vibrant energy below, creating a symbiotic dance between earthly celebrations and cosmic revelations.

Amid the solstice revelry, James Reed became not just a celebrant of traditions but a conduit for the cosmic forces that stirred beneath the surface. Unbeknownst to him, his infectious enthusiasm and magnetic charisma were threads woven into the cosmic fabric, contributing to the intricate patterns of a celestial design that transcended the boundaries of the ordinary.

As the town reveled in the solstice festivities, the Starry Haven observed from afar, its telescopes aimed at the cosmic canvas above. Driven by her insatiable curiosity, Dr. Victoria Monroe felt the pulse of cosmic energies intensify. The celestial dance between James's earthly charisma and the cosmic forces hinted at a revelation that would unfold as the winter solstice reached its zenith. The Town Center, aglow with festive lights and laughter, became a stage where earthly celebrations and cosmic mysteries converged, setting the scene for a night that would be remembered in the annals of eldritch Yuletide lore.

In the quiet confines of the Town Observatory, Dr. Victoria Monroe peered through the lenses of her telescope, the night sky reflecting in her determined eyes. Her passion for unraveling the mysteries of the cosmos led her to meticulous observations, and as she scrutinized the celestial canvas, a revelation unfolded before her.

Amidst the tapestry of stars, Dr. Monroe discerned an alignment of celestial bodies—an astronomical phenomenon not witnessed for centuries. In their cosmic ballet, the planets were choreographing a dance that coincided with the winter solstice, creating a celestial spectacle of unparalleled proportions.

The alignment, predicted by Dr. Monroe's keen astronomical acumen, held a significance that surpassed the understanding of the townsfolk engrossed in their solstice revelry. The cosmos had chosen this particular Yuletide night to unveil a celestial display that transcended the ordinary laws of planetary motion.

Excitement gripped Dr. Monroe as she deciphered the cosmic patterns, her findings hinting at a convergence of forces that bridged the gap between the earthly and the celestial. The alignment promised to infuse the winter solstice with otherworldly energy, amplifying the cosmic revelations already underway in the heart of the festive town.

As she meticulously documented her astronomical discovery, Dr. Monroe felt a sense of anticipation building within her. The celestial alignment, coinciding with the winter solstice, could unlock secrets buried in the depths of cosmic history. Unbeknownst to the townsfolk immersed in their solstice celebrations, the alignment signaled the beginning of a cosmic symphony, each celestial note resonating with the energies that permeated the Yuletide air.

With its telescopes aimed at the heavens, the Town Observatory became a silent witness to the unfolding cosmic drama. Dr. Monroe's revelation added an unseen layer to the festivities, as the astronomical discovery promised to elevate the winter solstice from a night of joyous celebration to a cosmic event that would leave an indelible mark on the town's collective memory.

In the heart of the Town Center, the air was charged with festive energy as townsfolk gathered to celebrate the winter solstice. James Reed, the charismatic orchestrator of the solstice revelry, infused the night with infectious enthusiasm. Decorations adorned the streets, and the vibrant hues of flickering lanterns painted a lively mosaic against the winter backdrop.

Unaware of the impending celestial alignment, the townspeople reveled in the solstice celebrations. Families strolled through the square, enjoying the warmth of bonfires and children's laughter echoing in the crisp winter air. Vendors lined the streets, offering delectable treats and trinkets that added to the joyous atmosphere.

Amidst the traditional festivities, there was a subtle undercurrent of anticipation—a collective excitement that transcended the ordinary. Unbeknownst to the celebrants, the cosmic energies already at play intertwined with the merriment, creating a harmonious blend of earthly delights and celestial wonders.

As the clock ticked closer to the predicted alignment, the celestial hub at the Town Observatory became a beacon for those attuned to the mysteries of the cosmos. Dr. Victoria Monroe's revelation, though known to only a select few, cast a subtle veil of cosmic significance over the solstice celebrations.

The celestial sleigh ride, the cosmic ornaments, and the impending alignment—each element wove together, creating a tapestry of eldritch mysteries that hovered just beyond the veil of perception. The solstice celebrations, vibrant and filled with the warmth of community, provided the perfect backdrop for the cosmic revelations set to unfold.

Amid the festivities, the celestial pilot observed with inscrutable eyes, aware that the solstice celebrations were but a prelude to the cosmic symphony about to engulf the town. The vibrancy of the winter solstice formed a delicate contrast to the cosmic forces steadily converging, promising a Yuletide night where the ordinary and the extraordinary would seamlessly intertwine.

In the dimly lit confines of the Town Observatory, Dr. Victoria Monroe, with an unwavering dedication to unraveling the mysteries of the cosmos, peered through the lenses of her telescope. The celestial tapestry above unfolded in a breathtaking display, stars waltzing in the vast expanse of the night sky.

Yet, as Dr. Monroe meticulously tracked the impending celestial alignment, a sudden shiver raced down her spine. The telescope, a conduit to the cosmic wonders, seemed to unveil more than the anticipated alignment—a foreboding vision, an eldritch twist to the cosmic ballet she had long studied.

Her eyes widened as she witnessed an ethereal dance of cosmic energies intermingling with the vibrant solstice celebrations below. The revelry took on an otherworldly hue, and the celestial alignment, rather than a mere astronomical event, became a conduit for eldritch forces to weave themselves into the fabric of the festivities.

Dr. Monroe, committed to empirical inquiry, was caught in the delicate balance between scientific curiosity and an unnerving revelation. Usually distant and indifferent, the cosmic energies now cast an ominous shadow over the solstice celebrations. It was as if the celestial alignment had opened a conduit to realms beyond, allowing eldritch forces to stir the essence of the winter solstice.

The foreboding vision lingered in Dr. Monroe's thoughts, leaving her with a profound sense of unease. As she grappled with the implications of what she had witnessed, the winter solstice festivities in the Town Center continued unabated, the townspeople unaware of the cosmic undercurrents that threatened to reshape their joyous celebrations into a cosmic spectacle.

The night sky over the Town Center underwent a profound transformation as the celestial alignment reached its zenith. The anticipated astronomical event, once a symbol of cosmic harmony, now heralded an uncanny eclipse that cast otherworldly shadows upon the quaint streets.

The townspeople, immersed in the solstice celebrations, began to notice the strange interplay of light and shadow. The festive decorations, once vibrant and full of life, now took on an ethereal glow, their colors warped by the celestial alignment. The towering Christmas tree in the center of the square, adorned with twinkling lights, became a surreal beacon against the eerie backdrop of cosmic shadows.

As the celestial forces reached their crescendo, the boundaries between the cosmic and the mundane blurred, and the air shimmered with eldritch energy. Otherworldly shadows danced along the edges of the festivities, creating an unsettling juxtaposition of joyous revelry and cosmic intrigue.

Unaware of the cosmic forces at play, the revelers continued to dance and celebrate beneath the celestial spectacle. Laughter echoed through the night, mingling with the subtle whispers of the cosmic energies that now permeated the atmosphere. The solstice celebrations, once a beacon of tradition and merriment, had become a stage for the cosmic and earthly convergence.

As the eerie eclipse unfolded, the townspeople remained oblivious to the cosmic shadows that clung to the edges of their reality. Unseen forces, drawn by the celestial alignment, observed the festivities with an inscrutable gaze, waiting for the cosmic revelations to unfold in the remaining nights of Eldritch Yule.

Amidst the celestial shadows that wove through the solstice celebrations, James Reed, the charismatic orchestrator of the festivities, was unknowingly entwined with cosmic energies. As he led the town in song and dance, his infectious enthusiasm and boundless energy unwittingly forged a cosmic bond between the earthly revelry and the eldritch forces that lingered in the shadows.

The cosmic bond strengthened with every beat of the festive music and every cheer that echoed through the Town Center. As the celebrant, James became a living conduit for the intermingling energies, a bridge between the joyous traditions of the solstice and the cosmic mysteries that lay beyond.

Unaware of the cosmic forces at play, James reveled in the solstice celebrations, his laughter and gestures amplifying the cosmic resonance. The celestial shadows, now imbued with the essence of the festivities, seemed to respond to his every movement, casting intricate patterns that mirrored the rhythm of the cosmic dance.

As the night progressed, the cosmic bond deepened, and James unwittingly became a central figure in the unfolding cosmic drama. The townspeople, caught in the mirth of the solstice revelry, remained blissfully ignorant of the unseen forces that intertwined with their celebrations.

The cosmic bond, once dormant, now pulsed with a quiet intensity, setting the stage for the nights ahead. The unwitting link between the earthly and the cosmic James Reed stood at the heart of a cosmic revelation that promised to transcend the boundaries of Midwinter's Eclipse.

The celestial alignment reached its zenith, and with it, the cosmic revelations unfolded like an ancient tapestry, revealing its intricate patterns. Realms began to merge, the earthly and cosmic boundaries becoming fluid and indistinct. It was as if unseen threads wove through the fabric of reality, binding the town's solstice celebration with cosmic energies beyond comprehension.

As the cosmic tapestry unfurled, celestial entities materialized, their forms ethereal and radiant against the backdrop of the eclipse. The festive lights of the Town Center shimmered alongside the cosmic luminance, creating a mesmerizing display that transcended the expectations of the solstice revelers.

The merging of realms became palpable as cosmic energies intermingled with the joyous atmosphere of the celebration. Still immersed in the festivities, Revelers began to feel a subtle shift. This resonance echoed the cosmic harmonies now playing out in the unseen dimensions. Laughter and merriment intertwined with ethereal whispers, creating a symphony that resonated across the earthly and the celestial planes.

The celestial entities, guardians of cosmic secrets, gracefully moved among the townspeople; their presence was felt but not fully understood. Their radiant presence added an otherworldly aura to the celebration, elevating it to a cosmic spectacle surpassing mortal imagination's limits.

As the realms continued to merge, the cosmic and the mundane danced in a delicate balance. The celestial entities, emissaries of the unknown, observed the revelry with inscrutable gazes, their motives hidden in the cosmic currents that now enveloped the town.

The merging of realms set the stage for an unprecedented cosmic drama, promising nights of Eldritch Yule where the boundaries between the seen and the unseen would blur, revealing the cosmic wonders that awaited in the celestial tapestry of Midwinter's Eclipse.

The eclipse began to wane as the celestial alignment concluded, and the cosmic energies intermingled with the winter solstice festivities gradually subsided. The ethereal shadows cast by the eclipse retreated, and the celestial entities gracefully faded from view, their otherworldly presence leaving an indelible mark on the townspeople's memories.

In the aftermath, the town stood in awe, absorbing the residual cosmic resonance in the air. It was as if the very fabric of the universe had momentarily brushed against the earthly realm, leaving behind a subtle echo that resonated in the hearts and minds of those who had witnessed the cosmic spectacle.

Though uncertain of the full extent of the cosmic forces at play, the townspeople felt a lingering connection to something beyond the ordinary. The solstice revelers, who unknowingly participated in merging realms, found themselves forever marked by the experience. The Town Center's festive lights now dimmed compared to the cosmic luminance they had witnessed, held a renewed significance—a testament to the cosmic mysteries that unfolded during Midwinter's Eclipse.

The residual cosmic resonance became a shared memory, a secret whispered among the townspeople who had been part of the cosmic revelation. In hushed conversations, they spoke of a night when the boundaries between the known and the unknown blurred, and the town became a celestial stage for a cosmic drama beyond mortal comprehension.

As the echoes of the cosmic resonance settled, the town prepared for the subsequent Yuletide nights, anticipating the continuation of the eldritch wonders that had begun to unfold. The cosmic tapestry, once glimpsed during the Midwinter's Eclipse, promised further revelations as the twelve nights of Eldritch Yule unfolded, each night holding the potential for cosmic mysteries to weave their intricate threads into the fabric of the town's collective destiny.

The Astral Nutcracker

The Bellamy Residence stood as a beacon of warmth amid the winter's chill, its interior adorned with twinkling lights and festive decorations. The aroma of holiday spices filled the air, creating a cozy haven for the family. Amid the traditional trappings of Christmas, a sense of anticipation lingered, as if the walls held secrets waiting to be unveiled.

In the heart of the Bellamy home, a portal to an enchanted ballet hall manifested—an ethereal space that existed beyond the boundaries of the mundane. Unaware of the magical doorway concealed within their residence, the family continued their holiday preparations, unsuspecting of the cosmic ballet that awaited them.

The enchanted ballet hall, hidden from the naked eye, was a realm where the Nutcracker's tale took on a celestial resonance. Reality seemed to warp within its confines as if the very essence of the holiday ballet transcended the ordinary and merged with eldritch energies.

As the Bellamy family went about their festive activities, little did they know that the Nutcracker, a timeless figure in holiday lore, would soon become a conduit for cosmic forces. Traditionally associated with dreams and enchantment, the ballet was about to take an otherworldly turn, intertwining the season's magic with cosmic mysteries that awaited their revelation.

The cozy holiday home and the hidden ballet hall were poised on the precipice of a cosmic performance—one where the Nutcracker's dance would echo through the realms beyond, resonating with the eldritch energies that had begun to weave their intricate threads through the tapestry of Eldritch Yule. The Bellamy family, drawn into the celestial ballet, would soon find themselves participants in a dance that transcended the boundaries of reality, where each pirouette and leap carried the weight of cosmic significance.

Within the Bellamy family, Clara, a ballet enthusiast with a heart of passion, found herself inexplicably drawn into the cosmic retelling of the Nutcracker's tale. Little did she know that her love for the ballet and her connection to the enchanting ballet hall within her home would make her a pivotal player in the unfolding events of this Eldritch Yule.

Amidst the festive season, a cryptic figure emerged in the guise of Major General George Drummond. His military background hid a complex network of secrets intricately woven with the cosmic forces that had selected the tale of the Nutcracker as their means of communication with the human world. Usually, a story of dreams and metamorphosis now bore the weight of concealed truths and revelations from beyond our world.

As Clara delved deeper into the ballet, the celestial resonance of the Nutcracker's tale became palpable. The enchanted ballet hall, hidden within the fabric of reality, pulsated with eldritch energies, casting an otherworldly glow on the performers and their audience. Every pirouette and every note of Tchaikovsky's composition seemed to echo through the cosmic corridors, resonating with the secrets held within Major General Drummond's enigmatic past.

The dance unfolded as a sequence of graceful movements and a cosmic performance that bridged the realms of dreams and the unknown. Clara, guided by her passion for ballet, found herself entangled in a cosmic dance that transcended the boundaries of the ordinary. With his military precision and concealed knowledge, Major General Drummond played a role beyond the confines of mortal understanding.

The Nutcracker's tale, once a charming fable of holiday enchantment, had become a conduit for cosmic forces—a story in which each step and each revelation echoed with the resonance of the eldritch. As the dance reached its climax, Clara and Major General Drummond stood at the forefront of a celestial spectacle, the Nutcracker's tale now a cosmic ballet that blurred the lines between fantasy and reality, ushering in the mysteries of the Astral Nutcracker.

Amidst the twinkle of festive lights and the aroma of holiday treats, the Bellamy Residence emerged as a haven of familial warmth and holiday cheer. Decorated with care, each corner exuded the spirit of the season, but it was in the heart of Clara Bellamy that a particular flame burned brightest—the flame of her love for ballet.

The living room, adorned with garlands and ornaments, became a cozy space where the family gathered to share laughter and create cherished memories. The fireplace crackled, casting a warm glow that danced upon the walls, echoing the joy that filled the air during the Eldritch Yule. Tucked beneath the Christmas tree were carefully wrapped presents, each holding the promise of delight and surprise.

Amidst this festive abode, Clara's passion for ballet found its place of honor. The walls echoed with the strains of classical music, and framed posters of renowned ballet performances adorned her room. A collection of ballet slippers, each pair telling a story of countless rehearsals and performances, lined the shelves, a testament to Clara's dedication to the art form.

As the Eldritch Yule festivities unfolded, Clara's love for ballet became a thread woven into the fabric of the holiday celebrations. With its enchanting ballet sequences, the Nutcracker's tale held a particular resonance for her. Little did she suspect that her passion would become a gateway to cosmic mysteries, drawing her into a dance that transcended the boundaries of the ordinary and embarked on a journey into the unknown realms of the Astral Nutcracker.

Clara's days were steeped in the graceful artistry of ballet, her passion flowing like a river of dance that coursed through her every step and heartbeat. Her enchantment with the Nutcracker's tale became a defining moment in her love for art. This annual tradition unfurled like the delicate petals of a winter bloom.

From a young age, Clara had been captivated by the elegance and precision of ballet. Her eyes would sparkle with anticipation as the Eldritch Yule season approached, heralding the time for the enchanting Nutcracker ballet. Year after year, she would join her family in the cozy living room, the glow of festive lights casting a warm embrace over the room. As the overture played, Clara would be transported into a world where the magic of dance and the allure of cosmic mysteries collided.

The performance, a celestial dance between the mundane and the eldritch, held Clara in rapt fascination. The Nutcracker's tale unfolded like a cosmic ballet, each pirouette and arabesque a step closer to the mystical realms beyond the veil of reality. Clara's passion for ballet, nurtured by these annual traditions, became a lantern guiding her through the dance of life.

Little did Clara know that this Eldritch Yule would bring more than just the annual Nutcracker performance—it would beckon her into an enchanted ballet hall hidden within the folds of reality, where cosmic forces awaited, ready to waltz with her through the Astral Nutcracker's celestial tale.

The snow-laden streets of Eldritch Yule whispered with anticipation as Major General George Drummond stepped into the quaint town. His arrival, shrouded in an enigmatic aura, aligned perfectly with the festive season, creating an unspoken intrigue that rippled through the community.

Dressed in a coat that seemed to bear the weight of secrets and adorned with a hat casting shadows over his eyes, Major General Drummond moved through the town like a figure from a tale untold. The locals exchanged curious glances, their hushed conversations veering toward speculation about the mysterious guest who had chosen to grace their town with his presence.

The Bellamy Residence, with its festive decorations and the echo of ballet music emanating from within, caught the attention of Major General Drummond. The allure of the Nutcracker's tale, intertwined with cosmic energies, beckoned him like a siren's call. As he approached the residence, the air grew heavy with the sense that his arrival was not a mere coincidence but a thread woven into the cosmic tapestry of Eldritch Yule.

The enigmatic guest, Major General Drummond, stood on the threshold of the festive abode, his presence casting a shadow that seemed to extend beyond the boundaries of the cozy home. Little did Clara and her family know that his arrival would set in motion a sequence of events that would blur the lines between the ordinary and the cosmic, transforming their Eldritch Yule into a celestial ballet of unforeseen wonders?

Beyond the threshold of the Bellamy Residence, Clara found herself stepping into a realm that transcended the ordinary. Following Major General Drummond's mysterious wake, she entered an enchanted ballet hall that defied the laws of reality. The air shimmered with cosmic energies, and the Nutcracker's tale unfolded in a dance of otherworldly grace.

The ballet hall was illuminated in celestial hues belonging to another world. Clara's eyes widened with amazement as the players from The Nutcracker, who were once confined to the stage, now appeared as ethereal beings. Their movements were guided by the cosmic forces that pulsed through the very fabric of the space, stretching into unseen dimensions.

As Clara looked up, she saw the Nutcracker standing tall and strong, guarding the eldritch ballet. She felt a deep connection with the dancers of this celestial performance, sensing a cosmic resonance. The music playing in the background was not produced by any earthly instrument. Still, its echo filled the entire hall, resonating with the hidden rhythms of the cosmos.

As Clara twirled and leaped alongside the enchanting figures, she became a part of a cosmic ballet. This astral performance reached beyond the boundaries of her understanding. Major General Drummond observed silently, his presence weaving into the dance, adding an air of mystery to the unfolding spectacle.

In this ethereal ballet hall, where the Nutcracker's tale melded with Eldritch's energies, Clara danced on the edge of reality, her every movement a step into the cosmic unknown. Little did she fathom that this cosmic journey would lead her to unravel mysteries that stretched far beyond the enchanting confines of Eldritch Yule.

The Nutcracker's story unfolded with a celestial twist as the otherworldly music filled the cosmic ballet hall. Enchanted dancers, their movements guided by cosmic forces, weaved a tale that transcended reality's boundaries. Now a participant in this astral ballet, Clara was entangled in a plot that unfolded like a cosmic tapestry.

The Nutcracker, once a wooden figure on a stage, took on a life of its own, embodying the spirit of Yuletide and Eldritch's mysteries. The enchanting dancers, each a manifestation of cosmic energies, twirled and leaped in a choreography that echoed through unseen dimensions.

The tale unfurled with a cosmic resonance, revealing realms beyond the veil of ordinary perception. Eldritch landscapes materialized, their ethereal beauty adding a surreal quality to the familiar Nutcracker's story. Mesmerized by the unfolding spectacle, Clara felt the pulsating energies of the cosmic dance resonating within her.

The story came to life in this ethereal ballet, pulsating with the spirit of Yuletide magic and cosmic wonders. Once a mere spectator of the Nutcracker's yearly spectacle, Clara now found herself an integral part of a plot that transcended the mundane and embraced the otherworldly.

As the cosmic dancers pirouetted and leaped, Clara realized that this enchanted ballet was more than a performance—it was a journey into the heart of Yuletide mysteries, where the Nutcracker's tale became a cosmic symphony, echoing through the cosmos and leaving an indelible mark on the fabric of Eldritch Yule.

As Clara watched the dancers in the astral ballet, she felt an inexplicable transformation. She no longer felt like a spectator but as if she was a ballet protagonist - a bridge between the earthly and the astral realms. The cosmic connection enveloping her blurred the boundaries between performer and audience. It was as if the dance recognized her as an essential part of the story that was unfolding.

As Clara watched the dancers in the astral ballet, she felt an inexplicable transformation. She no longer felt like a spectator but as if she was a ballet protagonist - a bridge between the earthly and the astral realms. The cosmic connection enveloping her blurred the boundaries between performer and audience. It was as if the dance recognized her as an essential part of the story that was unfolding.

With each graceful movement and ethereal pirouette, Clara felt the cosmic energies coursing through her, intertwining with the traditional Nutcracker's tale. She became a bridge between the ordinary and the extraordinary, a living embodiment of the eldritch forces that infused the ballet hall.

As she twirled with the enchanted dancers, Clara sensed the gaze of unseen cosmic entities, observers of this celestial ballet. The lines between the roles of dancer and observer blurred, and the distinction between reality and astral realms became a delicate dance in itself.

The astral ballet unfolded with Clara at its center, a cosmic protagonist embracing the mysteries of Eldritch Yule. The Nutcracker's tale, now interwoven with Clara's cosmic journey, resonated through the astral dimensions, creating a harmony that echoed beyond the confines of the enchanted ballet hall.

In this ethereal dance, Clara discovered that the cosmic connection forged in the astral realms went beyond the limits of perception. She became an integral part of a story that transcended the ordinary, embracing the eldritch wonders of the Yuletide cosmos.

Amidst the celestial dance, Major General Drummond stepped forward, a figure draped in mystery and revelation. With an air of solemnity, he began to unravel the cosmic forces that governed the enchanted ballet. His words were a tapestry woven with secrets, each thread connecting him to the eldritch mysteries that swirled within the astral ballet hall.

In a hushed tone, Major General Drummond disclosed his ancient lineage, one entwined with celestial entities that had long observed the earthly realms. He spoke of an otherworldly pact forged in the epoch's past, which bound his family to the cosmic forces that now manifested in the ballet's ethereal performance.

As he shared his connection to the eldritch mysteries, the dancers moved with a newfound intensity, their steps resonating with the cosmic revelations. Major General Drummond's presence became a focal point, a nexus between the mundane and the celestial as if his words were a key unlocking the secrets of the astral ballet.

The cosmic revelation deepened, transcending the confines of the enchanted ballet hall. Major General Drummond's disclosure echoed through the astral realms, intertwining with the dance, creating a harmonious symphony of eldritch energies. Still a participant in this cosmic tale, Clara felt the weight of ancient knowledge settling upon her as if the fabric of reality shifted under the influence of celestial truths.

Amid this cosmic unveiling, the ballet continued, now charged with a transcendent energy that pulsed through each movement. Major General Drummond, a keeper of cosmic secrets, stood as a sentinel at the intersection of realms, guiding the astral ballet toward an unknown cosmic crescendo.

The ethereal dancers transformed before Clara's wide eyes as the astral ballet unfolded. No longer bound by the limitations of human form, they became vessels for eldritch entities that transcended the boundaries of the earthly realm. Each pirouette and arabesque seemed to summon cosmic forces, manifesting as tendrils of astral energy that intertwined with the dancers' movements.

These astral entities, cloaked in otherworldly brilliance, brought a sublime terror that danced hand in hand with beauty. Their forms were ever-shifting, a kaleidoscope of celestial hues that defied the understanding of mortal eyes. Caught amid this cosmic ballet, Clara felt a chill run down her spine as the boundary between awe and trepidation blurred into a surreal symphony.

The astral dancers moved with an eerie grace, their steps echoing through the enchanted ballet hall like whispers from distant galaxies. With each leap and twirl, they wove a tapestry of eldritch energies, casting a spell that transported Clara beyond the known realms of perception. The dance became a mesmerizing blend of elegance and cosmic dread. This experience transcended the ordinary boundaries of human emotion.

As the astral entities continued their ballet, the very fabric of reality seemed to tremble. Clara's heart quickened, resonating with the pulsating energies from the cosmic dance. She became an unwitting witness to the convergence of worlds, where the astral and the corporeal coexisted in a delicate balance, threatening to unravel the threads of reality.

In the astral ballet's embrace, Clara stood at the threshold of the unknown, caught in the dance of eldritch entities that whispered secrets of cosmic significance. The astral dancers, embodiments of celestial mysteries, beckoned her to join their unearthly performance, inviting her to become a participant in the cosmic choreography that unfolded in the Enchanted Ballet Hall.

Amid the astral ballet's enchanting dance, Clara felt a subtle but profound shift within herself. The cosmic energies swirling around her seemed to permeate her very being, triggering a metamorphosis that transcended the boundaries of mortal understanding. Clara's senses underwent a cosmic recalibration as the astral entities continued their ethereal performance.

Colors took on hues beyond the spectrum of earthly perception, and sounds resonated with frequencies that echoed through unseen dimensions. Clara's vision expanded, allowing her to perceive the intricate interplay of cosmic forces that pulsed through the ballet hall. The astral dancers, once enigmatic entities, became conduits of cosmic wisdom, and Clara found herself attuned to the celestial symphony that accompanied their movements.

During a cosmic transformation, Clara felt a merging of her essence with the vast tapestry of the universe. She became a vessel for eldritch insights, her consciousness expanding beyond the confines of the mortal mind. The boundaries between self and cosmos blurred. Clara sensed the threads of destiny weaving a story far beyond the ballet's enchanting performance.

Clara's perception of reality profoundly transformed as the astral ballet reached its zenith. She saw the hidden connections that bound the Nutcracker's tale to the cosmic forces that governed the universe. The enchanted ballet hall became a focal point for revelations. Clara, now a participant in the cosmic dance, embraced the unfolding truths with a newfound awareness.

The cosmic metamorphosis gave Clara the gift of understanding—an insight into the intricate dance of cosmic forces that shaped the very fabric of existence.

With each movement of the astral dancers, Clara gleaned fragments of cosmic wisdom, unlocking the mysteries behind the veneer of ordinary reality.

In the aftermath of her cosmic metamorphosis, Clara stood in the Enchanted Ballet Hall, a conduit between the earthly and the astral. The Nutcracker's tale, now intertwined with her cosmic perception, became a key to unlocking the hidden truths of the eldritch mysteries awaiting subsequent Yuletide nights.

Clara emerged from the Enchanted Ballet Hall, the lingering echoes of the astral Nutcracker still resonating within her. As she stepped back into the warmth of the Bellamy Residence, the cosmic ballet's surreal memory clung to her consciousness like a delicate mist—a testament to an experience that transcended the bounds of the ordinary.

The festive decorations within the cozy holiday home took on a renewed vibrancy, their colors infused with traces of the cosmic palette Clara had witnessed in the astral realm. The Nutcracker's tale, now an indelible part of her cosmic perception, cast a celestial glow on the familiar surroundings.

Amidst the familial warmth and holiday cheer, Clara couldn't shake the ethereal tendrils of the astral Nutcracker's dance. It had become a cosmic thread woven into the fabric of her existence, a reminder of the eldritch mysteries that lay just beyond the veil of mundane reality.

As Clara reunited with the Bellamy Residence's festive ambiance, the astral Nutcracker's echoes lingered, a surreal memory shaping her understanding of the Yuletide nights to come. Little did she know that the cosmic revelations she had experienced were but a prelude to the cosmic wonders awaiting Eldritch Yule's subsequent nights.

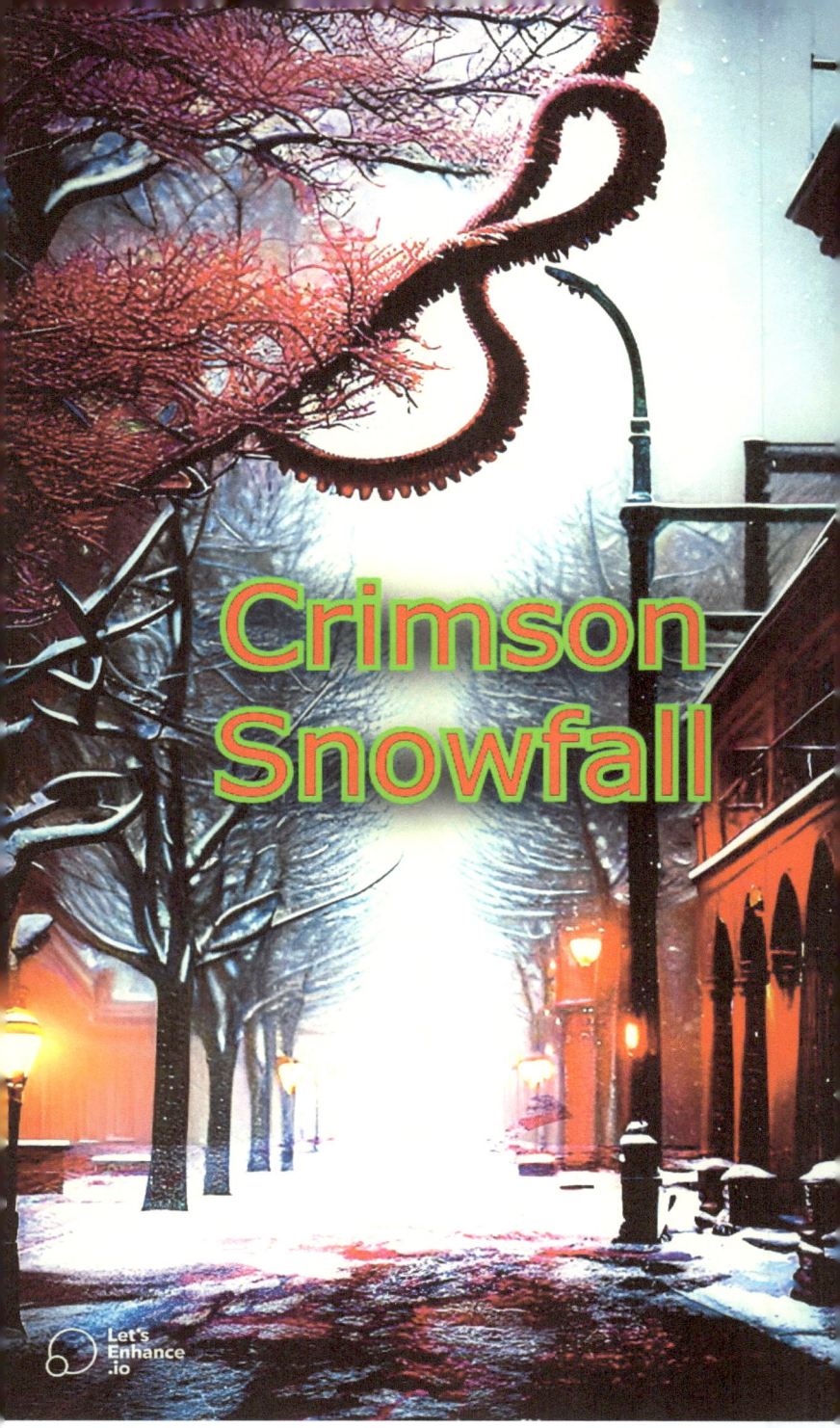

Crimson
Snowfall

Within the confines of the Whitman Residence, the warmth of familial bonds created a haven of anticipation and joy. Festive decorations adorned the cozy abode, casting a radiant glow that reflected the spirit of Christmas. Clara Whitman, the lead caroler, reveled in the cozy ambiance, her voice resonating with boundless enthusiasm as she prepared for the upcoming night of caroling in the Town Square.

The festive energy extended beyond the Whitman Residence into the heart of the village—the Town Square, a bustling hub of holiday activity. Decorative lights adorned buildings, and the air buzzed with the season's excitement. Unbeknownst to the villagers, the cosmic energies that had been stirred during the previous nights lingered, weaving unseen threads through the fabric of the festivities.

As Clara, with her unparalleled enthusiasm, led the carolers through the snowy streets, the cosmic influence began to manifest in subtle ways. The snowfall, once ordinary, took on a crimson hue, hinting at the eldritch forces seeping into the Yuletide celebrations. The villagers, caught in the festive fervor, remained oblivious to the cosmic transformation beneath the surface.

In the heart of the Town Square, where the community converged to celebrate, the cosmic tones introduced by Thomas Hayes during the Musical Prelude resonated once more. Clara's voice, a prelude to the cosmic drama, intertwined with Thomas's ethereal melodies, creating a harmonious blend that echoed beyond the audible, reaching out to the unseen forces that lingered in the winter air.

As the carolers continued their festive procession, the cosmic awakening unfolded. The joyous songs, unwittingly infused with cosmic resonance, became a beacon for unseen entities drawn to the celebration. The Frostbitten Transformation continued its subtle advance, with each snowflake imbued with cosmic energy, creating an otherworldly quality to the winter landscape.

Meanwhile, the silent violinist, Thomas Hayes, grappled with the unspoken connection to the cosmic energies stirred by his music. The Festive Procession, seemingly innocent on the surface, became a tapestry of cosmic forces interwoven with the villagers' merriment.

Unbeknownst to the carolers, Clara, the lead singer, unwittingly became the focal point for an unseen audience. Cosmic entities observed the festivities with inscrutable gazes, drawn to the harmonic convergence of joyous songs and ethereal melodies.

As the Threads of Cosmic Influence subtly unraveled the festive scene, the once-joyful celebration transformed into an unknowable cosmic spectacle. The echoes of the unknown lingered in the frostbitten air, setting the stage for the cosmic repercussions that would reverberate through subsequent Yuletide nights. The Whitman Residence and the Town Square, now entwined with cosmic energies, stood as witnesses to the unfolding cosmic drama, foreshadowing the mysterious events awaiting the coming nights.

As the cosmic tapestry unfolded in the Whitman Residence and the Town Square, the focus shifted to Dr. Isabella Hartfield, a meteorologist renowned for her expertise in atmospheric anomalies. Her cozy home, nestled on the outskirts of the village, provided a haven for scientific exploration adorned with weather instruments that echoed her fascination with the intricacies of the natural world.

Amid the festivities, Dr. Hartfield, with her analytical mind, couldn't ignore the subtle shifts in the atmosphere. The crimson snowfall, an anomaly that defied meteorological norms, captured her attention. Through the frost-laden windows of her observatory, she peered at the cosmic spectacle unfolding in the village.

Johnathan Whitman, patriarch of the Whitman family, embodied the festive spirit with unmatched enthusiasm. Little did he know that his unintentional role in the cosmic events would soon come to light. As Clara's father, he reveled in the joyous atmosphere, spreading warmth and merriment wherever he went.

Amid the celestial sleigh ride, the cosmic tones introduced by Thomas Hayes reached even Dr. Hartfield's meteorological instruments. Isabella, ever attuned to atmospheric nuances, detected harmonies beyond the audible—a cosmic resonance that merged with the winter air. As the celestial sleigh traversed the cosmic tapestry, leaving trails of ethereal magic, Dr.

Hartfield found herself drawn into the mysteries of the crimson snowfall.

The Threads of Cosmic Influence, woven by unseen entities, began to entwine with Dr. Hartfield's scientific curiosity. As she delved into her research, the celestial energies stirred by the cosmic awakening manifested in subtle atmospheric anomalies. The snowflakes, now imbued with cosmic energy, took on a mesmerizing dance, creating patterns mirrored the eldritch influence seeping into the festivities.

Unbeknownst to Dr. Hartfield, her meteorological observations became a critical factor in unraveling the enigma of the crimson snowfall. Guided by the festive spirit, Johnathan Whitman unknowingly played a role in the cosmic drama, becoming a focal point for the merging realms and celestial entities drawn to the village.

As the cosmic revelation during the Midwinter's Eclipse reverberated, Dr. Hartfield and Johnathan Whitman found themselves on the brink of a discovery. The mysteries of the crimson snowfall, intertwined with the festive celebrations, suggested a cosmic tapestry that went beyond human understanding. The stage was set for a cosmic drama, where science and the supernatural joined forces, creating a story that was difficult to fathom.

Amid the gently falling crimson snow, the Whitman Residence stood as a bastion of familial warmth, its walls adorned with festive decorations that shimmered in the ambient glow of hearth fires. The evergreen scent permeated the air as the family gathered to partake in the age-old tradition of decorating the Christmas tree.

Johnathan Whitman, the patriarch of the family, reveled in the joyous atmosphere. His infectious enthusiasm for the holidays echoed through the festively adorned halls, creating an ambiance of familial togetherness. The fireplace crackled, casting a comforting warmth that contrasted with the enchanting chill of the crimson snowfall outside.

In the heart of the Whitman Residence, the family exchanged laughter and shared stories, their bonds strengthened by the season's magic. The walls resonated with the merriment of children eagerly anticipating the arrival of Christmas morning. The Whitman home, nestled within the embrace of the cosmic winter, became a sanctuary of festive warmth.

As the evening unfolded, Isabella Hartfield, the inquisitive meteorologist, joined the Whitman family for the seasonal celebrations. The festive warmth enveloped her as she exchanged smiles and laughter with the Whitmans, momentarily setting aside her scientific inquiries to immerse herself in the joyous spirit of the holidays.

The air within the Whitman Residence hummed with the essence of familial love and the promise of Yuletide magic. Little did they know that, beyond the cozy confines of their home, the cosmic forces entwined with the crimson snowfall were weaving a tale that would leave an indelible mark on their festive celebrations. The stage was set for the unfolding cosmic drama, where the ordinary and the extraordinary coexisted in a dance of festive enchantment.

Dr. Isabella Hartfield, a seasoned meteorologist with a keen eye for atmospheric anomalies, gazed at the crimson snowfall with a scientist's curiosity. Her fascination with the skies had led her to dedicate her life to unraveling the mysteries of the ever-changing weather patterns. Still, tonight's crimson snowfall was unlike anything she had encountered before.

Isabella's meteorological instincts tingled as she observed the unique hue of the falling snow. Her mind, usually occupied with the mechanics of weather systems, now brimmed with questions about the cosmic forces at play. The scientist within her thirsted for knowledge, eager to decipher the enigma wrapped in the crimson veil that blanketed the town.

As the festivities continued within the Whitman Residence, Isabella stole moments to scrutinize the celestial display outside. Armed with her scientific curiosity, she contemplated the possible causes of the anomalous weather phenomenon. The crimson snow, she suspected, held secrets that transcended the boundaries of conventional meteorology.

The meteorologist's analytical gaze shifted from the festive warmth inside to the celestial canvas above.

The crimson snowfall, imbued with cosmic energies, hinted at a story beyond the grasp of earthly understanding. Little did she know that her scientific inquisitiveness would draw her deeper into the cosmic tapestry, where the celestial dance of snowflakes held a mystery that extended far beyond the realms of atmospheric science. The stage was set for Dr. Hartfield to embark on a journey into the unknown, where the boundaries between the scientific and the mystical blurred, and the crimson snow held the key to unraveling cosmic truths.

Johnathan Whitman, the patriarch of the Whitman family, moved through his festively adorned home with a buoyant spirit, his heart echoing with the joyful anticipation of Christmas. The air was infused with the scent of pine and the warmth of glowing hearth fires, creating a cozy haven for familial celebrations. Unbeknownst to Johnathan, cosmic forces stirred beyond the walls of his abode, weaving an intricate dance with the crimson snowfall that painted the town in otherworldly hues.

Johnathan reveled in the joyous atmosphere while preparing for the upcoming Christmas festivities. He engaged in the time-honored traditions of decorating the tree, hanging festive ornaments, and stringing lights illuminating the Whitman Residence like a beacon of holiday cheer. His infectious enthusiasm spread through the household, enveloping his family in the season's magic.

Little did Johnathan know that, as he embraced the festive warmth within the confines of his home, he stood at the nexus of cosmic energies. The crimson snowfall, a harbinger of eldritch wonders, whispered secrets that danced on the edges of perception. The patriarch's unwitting role in the unfolding cosmic tale would soon become apparent as the boundaries between the mundane and the mystical blurred, and the Whitman Residence transformed into a focal point for the convergence of cosmic forces.

As Johnathan continued to revel in the joyous anticipation of Christmas, the celestial ballet above wove a cosmic tapestry that would forever alter the course of his holiday celebrations. Unaware of the celestial spectacle unfolding outside, the Whitman family was on the brink of an extraordinary journey into the heart of the Eldritch Yule.

The ethereal phenomenon unfolded with the arrival of the crimson snowfall, casting a spell upon the town and its eager inhabitants. As the first delicate flakes descended from the cosmic realms, they painted the landscape in hues unseen by mortal eyes. The townsfolk, wrapped in the warmth of their holiday spirits, gazed in awe as the ethereal snowflakes danced through the air, leaving trails of eldritch brilliance in their wake.

With its otherworldly glow, the crimson snowfall transformed the town square into a mesmerizing tableau. Streets adorned with festive decorations now cradled the celestial cascade, turning the entire scene into a cosmic ballet. Initially taken aback by the unusual display, the townsfolk soon embraced the mystical ambiance, allowing the eldritch snow to become an integral part of their Christmas celebrations.

Children laughed and played, catching crimson snowflakes on their mittened palms, their faces illuminated by the ethereal glow. Vendors in the town square, their stalls adorned with seasonal treats, exchanged excited whispers about the enigmatic nature of the snowfall. Dr. Isabella Hartfield, a meteorologist with a keen eye for atmospheric anomalies, watched the phenomenon with scientific curiosity and a sense of wonder.

Amidst the festive atmosphere, Johnathan Whitman, unaware of the cosmic forces at play, joined the townsfolk in reveling in the crimson snowfall. The ethereal phenomenon had seamlessly woven into the fabric of the Christmas celebrations, creating a bridge between the mundane and the cosmic. As the town square sparkled with Eldritch's radiance, the stage was set for an unforgettable night, where the boundaries between reality and the unseen would blur even further.

Driven by scientific curiosity, Dr. Isabella Hartfield immersed herself in the pursuit of understanding the extraordinary crimson snowfall. As a dedicated meteorologist, she delved into the wealth of meteorological data, poring over charts, graphs, and historical records. Her observatory, usually a haven for stargazing, now transformed into a hub of scientific inquiry focused on unraveling the mysteries of this cosmic phenomenon.

Isabella meticulously analyzed the atmospheric conditions accompanying the crimson snowfall, searching for rational explanations to elucidate its origin. Yet, as she sifted through the data, she couldn't shake the lingering feeling that this was no ordinary meteorological event. The cosmic anomalies entwined with the snowfall hinted at forces beyond the scope of conventional science.

The townsfolk, wrapped in the joyous festivities, remained oblivious to the scientific pursuit unfolding in the observatory. Isabella, however, felt a growing sense of urgency, compelled to uncover the cosmic secrets concealed within the crimson snow. As her investigation progressed, she discovered correlations between celestial alignments and the ethereal precipitation, adding a layer of complexity to the enigma.

The scientist in her craved answers, but the eldritch nature of the phenomenon eluded easy classification. Isabella found herself at the intersection of science and the arcane, navigating uncharted territories that challenged the very foundations of her understanding. Little did she know that her scientific journey would soon converge with the cosmic forces at play, ushering in revelations transcending the boundaries of empirical inquiry.

Amid the joyous preparations in the Whitman Residence, Johnathan Whitman, the unsuspecting family patriarch, found himself unwittingly drawn into a cosmic tapestry woven by the crimson snowfall. As he went about the festive arrangements, the ethereal flakes, each imbued with cosmic energies, danced around him, creating an invisible connection between the earthly celebrations and ancient cosmic entities.

Unaware of the cosmic forces at play, Johnathan reveled in the joyful anticipation of Christmas, his heart filled with familial warmth and the spirit of the season. The seemingly innocent crimson snow added an otherworldly touch to the festivities, its subtle influence seeping into the fabric of the holiday cheer.

Little did Johnathan know he had become a conduit for the cosmic energies in the crimson snow. With each step he took and every decoration he placed, the ancient forces stirred, entwining the earthly celebrations with the mysteries of the cosmos. The festive atmosphere became a vessel for eldritch energies, and the Whitman Residence, once a haven of warmth, now resonated with cosmic vibrations.

As the crimson snow continued to fall, the unwitting conduit, Johnathan Whitman, stood at the center of a convergence—festivities merging with cosmic forces, creating a spectacle that transcended the ordinary and beckoned the town towards a Midwinter's revelation. The cosmos, it seemed, had chosen this festive abode as the stage for its enigmatic dance, with Johnathan unwittingly playing the role of the cosmic conductor.

Once a picturesque addition to the festive landscape, the crimson snow began its cosmic alchemy. Each delicate flake underwent a gradual transformation, an alchemical dance that signaled the awakening of ancient cosmic entities. The town's streets now blanketed in this otherworldly snow, shimmered with an ethereal glow as if the fabric of reality was woven anew.

As Dr. Hartfield delved into her scientific inquiry, she uncovered the intricate patterns of the cosmic alchemy within the crimson snowfall. Meteorological data and cosmic anomalies intertwined, revealing a celestial symphony orchestrated by forces beyond human comprehension. Once ordinary, the very essence of the snow now pulsed with eldritch energies, resonating with the impending revelation.

Unseen to the townsfolk, the crimson snow acted as a conduit for cosmic alchemy. This process bridged the gap between the earthly and the astral. The very substance of the snow became a vessel, its transformation a precursor to the unveiling of ancient entities that slumbered in the cosmic depths.

As the cosmic alchemy continued, the snow-covered streets bore witness to a metamorphosis—a blending of the mundane and the cosmic, as the town stood on the threshold of a revelation that promised to transcend the boundaries of ordinary winter festivities. The celestial dance of the crimson snow, now charged with cosmic significance, foretold a tale that would leave an indelible mark on the town's history, forever altering the fabric of its reality.

The ethereal forms materialized within the crimson snow, weaving through the festive town square like unseen threads connecting the earthly and the cosmic. These cosmic entities, ancient and enigmatic, manifested in shapes and hues beyond mortal comprehension. Their presence intertwined with the joyous revelry of the townsfolk, creating a surreal blend of celebration and cosmic revelation.

As children laughed and twirled in the crimson snow, the ethereal forms danced in tandem, their movements echoing the rhythms of the celestial realms. The townspeople, caught in the enchantment of the cosmic spectacle, felt a subtle shift in the air. This otherworldly resonance resonated with the very heartbeat of the universe.

The cosmic entities, adorned in hues that defied earthly description, observed the festivities with a benevolent gaze. Their forms pulsed with eldritch energies, glowing the snow-covered landscape radiantly. The townsfolk, unwitting participants in this cosmic ballet, reveled in the harmonious convergence of the mundane and the astral.

As the ethereal forms continued to intertwine with the crimson snowfall, the earthly and cosmic boundaries blurred. It was a moment of transcendence, where the town square became a nexus of cosmic energies, a convergence point for ancient entities to partake in the joyous spirit of the Yuletide festivities.

The celestial dance of the crimson snow reached its zenith, leaving an indelible mark on the town's collective memory. Having shared in the revelry, the ethereal forms gradually dissipated into the cosmic tapestry, leaving the townsfolk with a lingering sense of wonder—a testament to the cosmic wonders that unfolded during this enchanting night of Eldritch Yule.

Amidst the revelry and cosmic spectacle in the town square, Dr. Isabella Hartfield delved into the scientific enigma of the crimson snowfall. Armed with meteorological data and a keen intellect, she began unraveling the cosmic origins concealed within the ethereal flakes.

In her makeshift laboratory, adorned with weather instruments and cosmic charts, Dr. Hartfield meticulously studied samples of the crimson snow. Each crystalline structure held secrets, and a revelation unfolded as she peered through the microscope. The snowflakes bore intricate patterns that mirrored celestial constellations, a cosmic code written in the frosty script of the cosmos.

Her research led her deeper into atmospheric anomalies and cosmic phenomena. Driven by scientific curiosity, Dr. Hartfield unearthed connections between the crimson snowfall and ancient entities long dormant in the cosmic tapestry. The very essence of the snow resonated with the eldritch forces she had only read about in obscure tomes.

As she collected her findings, a cosmic tale unfolded - one of interstellar energies converging on the festive town, utilizing the crimson snow as a conduit. The celestial entities, dormant for centuries, stirred in response to the festivities, their awakening manifesting in the vibrant hues of the snow.

Dr. Hartfield's scientific inquiry became a journey into the unknown, a quest to understand the cosmic alchemy that transformed the mundane into the extraordinary. The crimson snow, once a meteorological anomaly, now stood as a testament to the intricate dance between science and the cosmic mysteries that unfolded during this mystical Yuletide night.

As the last ethereal remnants of the crimson snowfall settled onto the ground, the town square descended into an unusual hush. The cosmic echoes, once interwoven with joyous revelry, now faded into an eerie silence, leaving behind a palpable sense of wonder and transformation.

Standing amidst the quiet aftermath, Dr. Isabella Hartfield gazed at the celestial remnants on her fingertips. The scientific enigma had unfolded, revealing cosmic secrets that transcended the boundaries of earthly understanding. Once focused solely on the tangible world, her eyes now held a glint of something otherworldly—a recognition of the cosmic forces that had woven into the fabric of this festive night.

Johnathan Whitman, the unwitting conduit of the cosmic energies, felt a resonance within him, a connection to realms beyond the stars. The festive warmth that had surrounded him now mingled with the lingering echoes of ancient entities, forever changing him. Unbeknownst to him, he had become a part of a cosmic dance, a participant in a celebration that spanned the vastness of the cosmos.

As the townsfolk slowly emerged from their stunned silence, they realized that this Christmas would forever be etched in their memories. The cosmic forces had graced their celebration, leaving behind a town transformed by the fusion of the mundane and the eldritch.

The crimson snowfall had dissipated, leaving no trace of its ethereal presence. Still, the cosmic echoes persisted in the hearts and minds of those who had witnessed the celestial spectacle. Dr. Hartfield and

Johnathan Whitman, representatives of science and festive spirit, stood side by side, forever bound by the cosmic forces that had chosen their town as the stage for this otherworldly performance.

In the heart of the Montgomery Residence, where the warmth of familial bonds melded with the festive spirit, a subtle sense of anticipation filled the air. The intimate family home, adorned with holiday decorations, became a haven for shared moments and cherished memories, oblivious to the cosmic forces about to unfold.

Meanwhile, the Charming Village Square, typically a picturesque scene of holiday cheer, took on an ethereal glow as cosmic energies converged upon it. Unbeknownst to the villagers, the square had become a stage for supernatural mischief, where the mystical mistletoe exerted its influence on relationships, creating excitement and trepidation.

As the Montgomery family gathered in their festively decorated home, the patriarch, Mr. Montgomery, prepared to hang the mistletoe in the doorway—a tradition passed down through generations. Little did they know that this seemingly ordinary sprig held otherworldly properties, poised to weave its cosmic magic among the village's inhabitants.

Friends and neighbors gathered in the Village Square, unaware of the subtle shifts in the cosmic tapestry above them. Laughter and joy echoed through the air as the cosmic mistletoe, invisible to the human eye, began its ephemeral dance, influencing the destinies of those who stood beneath its unseen influence.

As the night unfolded, relationships took unexpected turns, and emotions stirred beneath the celestial mistletoe's spell. The Village Square became a stage for cosmic connections, where the ordinary mingled with the extraordinary, and the ephemeral mistletoe left an indelible mark on those touched by its supernatural influence.

Elizabeth Montgomery was caught in the whirlwind of holiday preparations in the heart of the Montgomery Residence. The air was filled with the scent of pine and cinnamon, and the soft glow of fairy lights adorned every corner. As the protagonist of this cosmic tale, Elizabeth couldn't escape the complexities of relationships, and the imminent arrival of the ephemeral mistletoe added an unexpected layer to the holiday festivities.

Across the village, Thomas Campbell felt a subtle tug, a connection to the cosmic energies swirling around the mystical mistletoe. Unbeknownst to him, his presence in the Village Square held a significance that transcended the ordinary. The cosmic forces at play sought to intertwine the lives of those gathered. With his unseen connection, Thomas was a crucial player in this celestial drama.

As Elizabeth and Thomas crossed paths beneath the twinkling lights of the Village Square, the invisible influence of the cosmic mistletoe began to weave its magic. Laughter and conversations took on a subtle energy, relationships shifted, and the atmosphere crackled with a cosmic undercurrent.

Under the ethereal glow of the supernatural mistletoe, Elizabeth was drawn into conversations and moments that seemed guided by forces beyond her understanding. Thomas, too, experienced the cosmic influence, sensing a connection between himself and the ephemeral mistletoe that surpassed the boundaries of mere chance.

As the night unfolded, relationships in the Village Square became a tapestry of cosmic threads, intertwining and unraveling in patterns unseen. Elizabeth and Thomas, each navigating the cosmic currents in their own way, found themselves at the center of a celestial dance that promised mystery and revelation.

Once a charming backdrop for holiday festivities, the Village Square became a stage for the cosmic forces at play. As the ephemeral mistletoe continued its dance, the lives of Elizabeth Montgomery, Thomas Campbell, and the other villagers became intricately woven into the cosmic fabric of the Eldritch Yule, forever changed by the enchantment of the cosmic mistletoe.

Festive warmth permeated the air within the intimate confines of the Montgomery Residence. The crackling fireplace cast a comforting glow, and the walls echoed with the laughter of family members engaged in holiday preparations. The scent of freshly baked cookies and the sight of carefully adorned decorations created an atmosphere of joy and togetherness.

Elizabeth Montgomery found solace and excitement amid the bustling activities in this familial haven. The warmth of the holiday season enveloped her, and the anticipation of shared moments with loved ones heightened the sense of connection.

As the cosmic energies surrounding the ephemeral mistletoe began to stir, the Montgomery Residence became a focal point for the unfolding celestial drama. Unbeknownst to the family, the mistletoe held powers beyond the ordinary, and its influence would soon weave through the fabric of their relationships.

The decorations adorning the Montgomery home took on a subtle shimmer as the cosmic forces prepared to play their part. Little did the family know that beneath the surface of their festive traditions, a cosmic dance was about to unfold, guided by the unseen influence of the ephemeral mistletoe.

In the heart of this familial warmth, Elizabeth and her family members, unaware of the cosmic machinations at play, continued their preparations for the approaching holiday celebrations. The air buzzed excitedly, and the cosmic forces, dormant for so long, stirred with anticipation.

As the Montgomery Residence became a nexus for both earthly traditions and cosmic intrigue, the stage was set for the ephemeral mistletoe to work its celestial magic, leaving an indelible mark on the familial bonds and relationships that flourished within its warm embrace.

Amid the festive warmth of the Montgomery Residence, Elizabeth found herself navigating the intricate web of relationships that defined her world. Within the familial embrace, her connections with parents, siblings, and extended family members unfolded in a dance of shared memories and cherished moments.

The aroma of holiday meals, the laughter echoing through the halls, and the exchange of thoughtful gifts contributed to the tapestry of familial ties. Elizabeth's interactions with her parents revealed a deep bond rooted in love and shared traditions. At the same time, the camaraderie with her siblings carried the echoes of childhood mischief and sibling banter.

Beyond the familial sphere, Elizabeth's romantic entanglements added another layer of complexity to the holiday season. The delicate dance of affection and understanding played against twinkling lights and festive decorations. Moments of joy and shared laughter intertwined with the challenges of navigating the expectations that the season brought.

Unbeknownst to Elizabeth, the ephemeral mistletoe lingered overhead like a cosmic spectator, its subtle influence poised to weave through the threads of relationships. As the holiday festivities unfolded, the cosmic energies surrounding the mistletoe began to stir, adding an ethereal quality to the emotions that blossomed within the Montgomery Residence.

In the warmth of familial love and the embrace of romantic connections, Elizabeth found herself at the heart of a cosmic drama, where the ephemeral mistletoe held the power to amplify the joys and trials of the holiday season. Little did she know that the ties she navigated were about to be subtly influenced by forces beyond the realm of ordinary understanding, creating a tapestry of relationships woven with both earthly and cosmic threads.

In the quaint village square, where the essence of holiday cheer wafted through the air, a mysterious figure emerged from the periphery of the festivities. With an aura of enigma surrounding him, Thomas Campbell stepped into the vibrant scene of joyous celebrations.

The townsfolk couldn't help but look curious at the newcomer, whose arrival seemed almost serendipitous amidst the revelry. Dressed in attire that echoed a timeless elegance, Thomas moved with a measured grace as if choreographed by unseen forces.

As he strolled through the village square, festooned with twinkling lights and the aroma of holiday treats, Thomas became an unwitting participant in the cosmic drama orchestrated by the ephemeral mistletoe. Unbeknownst to him, the celestial energies surrounding the mistletoe sensed his presence, and a subtle cosmic resonance began to weave its influence into the tapestry of relationships.

Elizabeth, engaged in the festivities and unaware of the mistletoe's ethereal powers, found her path intersecting with Thomas's enigmatic journey. Their encounter, seemingly ordinary on the surface, carried the cosmic potential to shape the dynamics of the relationships blossoming within the village.

As the night unfolded and the cosmic energies stirred, the mysterious visitor and the ephemeral mistletoe became entangled in a dance of cosmic intrigue. The village square, illuminated by the glow of holiday lights, became the stage for a celestial performance that would leave an indelible mark on the relationships entwined in the festive warmth.

Little did the villagers know that, beneath the joyous celebrations, the cosmic forces at play were orchestrating a tale of connections, mysteries, and the ephemeral magic of the holiday season.

As the clock ticked towards midnight, the cosmic energies dormant within the ephemeral mistletoe began to stir. Unseen forces, beyond the comprehension of the villagers, unleashed a subtle yet potent influence that permeated the quaint village square.

Under the cosmic sway of the mistletoe, emotions became heightened, and the bonds between individuals were put to the test. Laughter echoed with a cosmic resonance, joy seemed to shimmer with an otherworldly glow, and even the most mundane interactions took on an ethereal quality.

In the soft glow of holiday lights, couples and friends were drawn into a dance of emotions guided by the celestial forces embedded in the mistletoe. Like invisible threads, the cosmic energies wove through the festive air, amplifying the warmth of familial ties and kindling the flames of romantic connections.

Unknowingly at the center of this cosmic spectacle, Elizabeth experienced a surge of emotions as she navigated the mingling crowds. The cosmic energies teased at the edges of her awareness, intertwining with the complexities of relationships and testing the resilience of the bonds she held dear.

As the night unfolded, the villagers, caught in the cosmic currents of the mistletoe's influence, were entangled in a web of emotions that transcended the ordinary. The supernatural properties of the mistletoe became a catalyst for revelations, confessions, and unexpected turns in the cosmic dance of connections.

Amid the festive warmth and twinkling lights, the village square transformed into a stage where cosmic energies played with the hearts and souls of those gathered. Little did they realize that, beneath the veneer of holiday cheer, the ephemeral mistletoe held the key to unlocking the celestial mysteries that bound their fates together.

Beneath the ancient boughs of the ephemeral mistletoe, the village square lay adorned with festive decorations, blissfully unaware of the otherworldly intrusion occurring in its midst. To the villagers, the mistletoe appeared as a quaint and ordinary emblem of holiday traditions, hanging innocuously overhead.

Unbeknownst to them, the seemingly mundane mistletoe harbored cosmic powers, woven into its very essence by forces beyond the veil of reality. The celestial energies it contained were dormant, patiently awaiting the arrival of the cosmic event that would awaken their influence.

As the clock struck midnight, a subtle shift occurred. The air around the mistletoe shimmered with a faint glow, imperceptible to the villagers engrossed in their joyous revelry. Unseen tendrils of cosmic energy extended from the mistletoe, reaching out like ethereal threads seeking connection.

Amid the festive warmth, the otherworldly intrusion unfolded silently. The mistletoe, a celestial conduit, became a bridge between the ordinary and the cosmic, its cosmic powers ready to influence the course of relationships and emotions in the village.

The villagers continued their merriment, unaware of the cosmic tapestry woven above them. The ephemeral mistletoe, now aglow with eldritch energies, stood as a harbinger of the surreal events that would unfold in the remaining nights of Eldritch Yule.

Under the celestial influence of the mistletoe, emotions in the village square began to amplify like ripples on a cosmic pond. Unspoken feelings surged to the surface, and the festive warmth took on an ethereal intensity. Laughter echoed with a touch of cosmic mirth, and smiles carried the weight of unspoken mysteries.

Couples stood beneath the glowing mistletoe, their shared glances suddenly charged with unexplored depths. The cosmic energies worked as an unseen force, weaving a tapestry of connections that transcended the ordinary dynamics of the village.

Familial ties, already strong in the festive atmosphere, faced the cosmic challenge. Joyous reunions held an undercurrent of cosmic tension as long-buried grievances resurfaced under the influence of the mistletoe's amplified emotions.

As the villagers navigated the intricate dance of amplified emotions, the ephemeral mistletoe became a silent witness to the cosmic alchemy at play. Unbeknownst to them, the seemingly innocuous plant served as a conduit for eldritch forces, testing the bonds between individuals and reshaping the intricate web of relationships in the village.

Beneath the soft glow of the mistletoe, Elizabeth found herself entangled in a cosmic ballet of emotions. The familiar bonds of family and the delicate threads of romance became intertwined, creating a tapestry of emotional turmoil.

Within the cosmic influence of the mistletoe, unresolved feelings and unspoken words surfaced, casting a surreal light on the complexities of familial ties. Joy and tension coexisted as Elizabeth navigated the delicate dance of emotions, her heart a battleground where cosmic forces played their enigmatic tune.

The festive warmth of the village square became a crucible of emotional transformation for Elizabeth. She faced the cosmic challenge head-on, confronting the depths of familial connections and the intricacies of romantic entanglements. The mistletoe, an unwitting catalyst for cosmic revelations, guided her through self-discovery amidst the amplified emotions that swirled around her.

As the ephemeral mistletoe continued to weave its cosmic influence, Elizabeth's emotional landscape shifted, leaving her forever changed by the cosmic forces that had chosen the village as their celestial stage. The echoes of her journey lingered in the air, a testament to the cosmic dance that unfolded under the seemingly ordinary guise of the festive mistletoe.

In the heart of the village square, Thomas Campbell emerged as a silent guardian of cosmic forces, his connection to the mistletoe's supernatural properties veiled in mystery. With an air of quiet authority, he observed the emotional tapestry woven by the celestial plant, understanding its role in testing the bonds between individuals.

A stoic figure amidst the swirling emotions, Thomas carried the weight of knowledge about the mistletoe's cosmic energies. His steady and perceptive gaze traced the ebb and flow of amplified feelings, acknowledging the profound impact of the otherworldly intrusion on the villagers.

As the guardian of cosmic forces, Thomas found himself entangled in the intricate dance of emotions, silently witnessing the amplified connections and tensions brought forth by the mistletoe. His enigmatic presence added a layer of cosmic significance to the unfolding events, hinting at a deeper understanding of the mystical energies at play.

Amid the village square's festive warmth, Thomas Campbell stood as a silent sentinel, a keeper of cosmic secrets, as the ephemeral mistletoe continued to amplify emotions and reshape the relationships that bound the villagers together. The guardian's role unfolded in tandem with the cosmic revelations, leaving an indelible mark on the tapestry of the Eldritch Yule.

The realization of unseen forces at play dawned upon Elizabeth and the villagers, a collective awareness transcending the mundane. As the cosmic energies embedded in the ephemeral mistletoe continued to weave their intricate web, relationships became battlegrounds and sanctuaries.

Under the celestial plant's influence, emotions intensified, revealing the unspoken depths of connections that had long lingered beneath the surface. Once unaware of the cosmic forces, the villagers found themselves navigating a landscape where sentiments were amplified, tested, and reshaped by the unseen hand of eldritch influence.

The ethereal mistletoe, seemingly innocuous yet harboring cosmic powers, became a focal point for turmoil and revelation. Bonds were strained, secrets unveiled, and unexpected alliances formed, all orchestrated by the unfathomable forces that now held sway over the village square.

Amid emotional turmoil, the villagers grappled with the cosmic dance set in motion by the mistletoe. Unseen forces guided their steps, challenging the very fabric of relationships while strengthening the ties that bound them together. As the cosmic influence unfolded, the village square became a stage for personal revelations and communal understanding, forever altered by the ephemeral mistletoe's enigmatic powers.

As the cosmic energies woven into the ephemeral mistletoe began to wane, a palpable shift settled over the Village Square. The once vibrant and tumultuous emotions, amplified by the unseen forces at play, gradually subsided, leaving behind a lingering sense of reflection.

The villagers, their hearts no longer under the enchantment of the cosmic dance, found themselves in a moment of collective introspection. Relationships, tested and reshaped by the mistletoe's influence, were now subject to contemplation and understanding. Witnessing turmoil and revelation, the Village Square stood as a silent testament to the cosmic forces that had briefly held sway.

Elizabeth and Thomas, forever changed by the celestial plant's enigmatic powers, now carried the echoes of emotions amplified and connections reshaped within them. Although fading, the ephemeral mistletoe's cosmic dance left an indelible mark on the village and its inhabitants. As the cosmic influence retreated, the Village Square became a space for introspection and reconciliation, a testament to the ephemeral nature of the mistletoe's otherworldly

influence.

The Candles of Time

Within the hallowed halls of Montgomery Clockworks, where the ceaseless ticking of intricate timepieces echoed through the air, a sanctum of ancient mechanisms and cosmic secrets unfolded. The Clockwork Sanctum, a haven of perpetual motion and hidden wonders, concealed within its gears the enigma of the candles that held the essence of time.

Amidst the ticking and whirring gears intertwined with cosmic energies, a hidden doorway emerged—an entryway to a realm beyond the ordinary flow of time. The Time-Traveler's Portal, nestled within the heart of Montgomery Clockworks, became the focal point for cosmic unraveling and manipulating time's delicate threads.

As the villagers, unaware of the cosmic machinations at play, went about their daily lives, the candles of time flickered within the Clockwork Sanctum, their flames dancing with the ebb and flow of temporal energies. The portal stood as a gateway to eternity, inviting those who dared to venture into the unknown realms of past and future.

In this clandestine setting, where the cosmic and the mechanical coalesced, the candles of time could shape destinies and unveil the mysteries hidden within the tapestry of existence. With its gears and celestial secrets, the sanctum whispered promises of temporal manipulation and journeys through the corridors of ages. The candles, aglow with the essence of time, awaited the touch of those destined to unravel the cosmic secrets veiled within Montgomery Clockworks.

In the dimly lit chambers of Montgomery Clockworks, Professor Reginald Montgomery, the custodian of temporal secrets, stood amidst the rhythmic cadence of ticking timepieces. His keen eyes, framed by years of wisdom, held the weight of knowledge about the cosmic candles that adorned the sanctum. Each candle, a sentinel of time's passage, whispered secrets of temporal mysteries to the venerable custodian.

Olivia Bennett, drawn by an unseen force, was entwined with the enigmatic events unfolding within the cosmic embrace of Christmas. Her connection to the candles remained mysterious, a subtle dance between fate and cosmic design that would unravel as the Christmas season unfolded.

As Professor Montgomery meticulously tended to the gears and mechanisms, he deciphered the arcane language of the candles—a countdown etched in cosmic symbols, signaling an impending convergence of temporal forces. The sanctum resonated with the hum of temporal energies and promised revelations that transcended the boundaries of mortal understanding.

Olivia, drawn by an irresistible pull, entered the Clockwork Sanctum, where the candles' flames flickered in synchronous rhythm with the cosmic heartbeat. The countdown, written in the language of celestial bodies, hinted at an event of cosmic proportions. This revelation would leave an indelible mark on the fabric of time.

Professor Reginald Montgomery and Olivia Bennett stood at the threshold of a cosmic journey in this hallowed space, where gears turned in harmony with cosmic energies. The candles, their flames casting shadows that danced across the walls of the sanctum, held the key to unlocking the secrets of time itself. The countdown continued, an ethereal echo in the timeless corridors of Montgomery Clockworks as the cosmic events of Eldritch Yule unfolded.

Within the echoing halls of Montgomery Clockworks, the air hummed with the resonant melody of time itself. The sanctum, a haven of temporal wonders, held within its gears and cogs the secrets of cosmic significance. Professor Reginald Montgomery, a guardian of the temporal tapestry, moved with a measured grace among the intricate timepieces that adorned the walls.

The ticking of clocks, synchronized with the heartbeat of the cosmos, created an atmosphere where time seemed to ebb and flow in harmonious unity. Each gear in the Clockwork Sanctum was a testament to Professor Montgomery's dedication to preserving the delicate balance between the mortal realm and the cosmic forces that governed it.

As Olivia Bennett stepped into this temporal haven, the ethereal glow of candle flames painted the space with an otherworldly luminescence. The countdown of the cosmic candles, etched in the fabric of time, resonated with the hum of ancient mechanisms. The sanctum was a testament to the interplay of celestial energies and mortal craftsmanship—a bridge between the known and the cosmic unknown.

Olivia and Professor Montgomery stood on the threshold of revelations in this haven, where past, present, and future coalesced. The candles, flickering in silent anticipation, were not mere instruments marking the passage of time; they held the power to unlock the mysteries of temporal existence.

Montgomery Clockworks, a sanctuary of cosmic secrets, pulsed with the heartbeat of ages. As the cosmic countdown continued, the destinies of those drawn into its embrace unfolded in a dance with the candles that transcended the ordinary bounds of time.

The candles, ancient timepieces with wicks that burned with cosmic flames, stood as silent sentinels within the intricate expanse of Montgomery

Clockworks. Each candle possessed an ethereal glow that defied the mundane, and their flames whispered the secrets of ages past and epochs yet to unfold.

Arranged in a celestial alignment, the candles became conduits of cosmic energies, their wax holding the imprints of events beyond mortal comprehension. The enigmatic countdown etched into each candle's surface was a language spoken by the cosmos—a rhythmic pulse resonating with the cosmic dance of stars.

As the candles flickered, their glow cast shadows that danced upon the walls, revealing glimpses of events shrouded in the veils of time. The air within the Clockwork Sanctum seemed to thicken with the weight of temporal significance, and the countdown of the candles became a hymn that echoed through the corridors of destiny.

Professor Montgomery, the custodian of these ancient timepieces, traced the contours of the candles with a reverence that transcended the ordinary. With its unique flame, each candle held a fragment of the cosmic narrative—a countdown to events that would weave the destinies of those touched by the eldritch yuletide.

Once drawn into this cosmic tapestry, Olivia Bennett felt the candles' resonance deep within her being. As mysterious as the stars themselves, the countdown beckoned her to unravel the threads of time and discover the cosmic secrets hidden within the flickering flames. Like beacons of ancient wisdom, the candles stood witness to the unfolding of an ephemeral yuletide where past, present, and future converged in a dance of celestial proportions.

Professor Montgomery, a venerable guardian of the candles, stood amidst the temporal wonders of

Montgomery Clockworks. His eyes, aged yet gleaming with wisdom, reflected the eons of knowledge etched into the very fabric of his being. The sanctum, enveloped in the hum of ancient gears and the soft ticking of myriad timepieces, bore witness to the custodian's solemn duty—safeguarding the candles that held the secrets of cosmic epochs.

With hands weathered by the touch of time, Professor Montgomery delicately adjusted the candles, his movements synchronized with the ethereal cadence of the cosmic countdown. His understanding of the cosmic forces that wove through the essence of time was profound, wisdom earned through years of communion with the celestial rhythms.

As the guardian, he bore the weight of temporal responsibilities, ensuring that the candles burned with the precise tempo required for the cosmic events to unfold harmoniously. His eyes, marked by the reflections of countless yuletides past, held a gaze that transcended the mundane, glimpsing the unseen threads that bound the candles to the fate of those touched by the eldritch yuletide.

Professor Montgomery's connection to the candles went beyond mere custodianship; it was a symbiotic relationship, a dance with the forces that governed the tapestry of time. He could decipher the subtle nuances of the countdown, interpreting the cosmic messages woven into the flickering flames.

In the silence of the Clockwork Sanctum, Professor Montgomery stood as a sentinel, his presence an anchor in the ever-shifting currents of temporal flux. The guardian of time, he guided the candles through the ages, an eternal steward of the cosmic secrets that unfolded beneath the celestial canopy of Eldritch Yule.

The brass bells above the entrance to Montgomery Clockworks jingled softly as Olivia Bennett stepped into the temporal haven. A cloak of mystery draped around her, woven with threads of cosmic intrigue that mirrored the ancient gears and timepieces surrounding her. With his watchful eyes, Professor Montgomery acknowledged her arrival with a nod, recognizing the unspoken connection that bound her to the celestial countdown of the candles.

Olivia's eyes, a deep well of secrets, scanned the intricate mechanisms of the clockworks with a familiarity that hinted at a cosmic understanding. The ticking and tocking of countless timepieces echoed in the chamber, a melodic backdrop to the unfolding enigma.

Approaching the candles, Olivia extended a hand, her fingers brushing the ethereal flames with a delicate reverence. The flickering dance responded, casting ephemeral shadows on her face as if whispering tales of cosmic epochs and eldritch mysteries. Her connection to the countdown was palpable, a silent communion between the mysterious visitor and the cosmic forces that threaded through the candles.

Professor Montgomery, his gaze a reflection of aged wisdom, observed Olivia with a mixture of curiosity and recognition. The temporal sanctum, once a haven solely guarded by him, now bore witness to the convergence of cosmic energies embodied in the enigmatic visitor.

As Olivia stood amid the timeless realm, the candles' flames seemed to synchronize with the pulse of her presence as if acknowledging her as a custodian of the cosmic secrets they harbored. The air within the sanctum hummed with a subtle resonance, echoing the profound connection between Olivia Bennett and the mysteries that unfolded with each passing moment.

In the heart of Montgomery Clockworks, two guardians of time—one seasoned by the ages, the other veiled in mystery—stood united by a shared purpose, their destinies entwined with the celestial countdown that heralded the unfolding cosmic tapestry of Eldritch Yule.

The candles within Montgomery Clockworks, ancient timepieces with cosmic souls, ignited with an ephemeral glow. The flickering flames, ethereal and spectral, cast an enchanting radiance that danced across the temporal haven. The air shimmered with the subtle energy of the cosmic countdown. This silent proclamation transcended the boundaries of conventional time.

As the candles began their celestial vigil, the room underwent a metamorphosis. The gears of the clockworks hummed in harmony with the cosmic forces, their rhythmic cadence merging with the otherworldly glow of the flames. The ephemeral flames held within them the essence of ages, a fusion of temporal mysteries that unfolded with each passing second.

The spectral glow intensified, casting intricate shadows on the walls adorned with ancient timepieces. The temporal haven resonated with the cosmic energies as if the very fabric of reality was woven into a tapestry of temporal wonders. The initiation of the cosmic countdown was a mesmerizing spectacle, a celestial overture to a symphony that echoed through the corridors of time.

Within this sanctum of ephemeral flames, Professor Montgomery and Olivia Bennett stood as witnesses to the cosmic ballet, their roles intertwined with the ancient candles that marked the passage of epochs. The temporal unraveling had commenced, and as the glow of the candles intensified, so did the enigmatic journey that awaited them—a journey through the veiled corridors of Eldritch Yule, where time would dance to the cosmic rhythm.

The spectral glow of the candles within Montgomery Clockworks intensified. As the cosmic countdown progressed, the room quivered with the release of space-time ripples. Anomalies surged through the temporal fabric, creating ephemeral windows into the vast past, present, and future expanse.

Within these ripples, scenes unfolded like fragments of a cosmic tapestry. Glimpses of bygone eras materialized—the echoes of ancient civilizations, long-forgotten landscapes, and the distant whispers of cosmic secrets. Temporal tendrils reached into the present, unveiling moments of significance and insignificance as if time played a symphony of interconnected events.

The future, veiled in uncertainty, teased the observers with fleeting glimpses of what might be. Like a cosmic dance, Destiny revealed itself in intricate patterns, and the space-time ripples became a kaleidoscope of potentialities. The room resonated with the harmonious chaos of past, present, and future converging in a celestial ballet.

Professor Montgomery and Olivia Bennett, standing amidst the undulating waves of space-time ripples, became witnesses to the cosmic tapestry that unfurled before them. With their enigmatic countdown, the candles were the catalysts for this temporal ballet, orchestrating a symphony of interconnected moments that transcended the conventional boundaries of time. The sanctum of Montgomery Clockworks had become a portal to the cosmic dance of space and time.

As the space-time ripples continued to weave their intricate patterns, Olivia Bennett found herself irresistibly drawn to the candles. Their ephemeral flames whispered secrets of cosmic origins and enigmatic powers, and a silent bond formed between Olivia and the temporal wonders.

Amid the unfolding cosmic dance, Olivia's latent abilities began to awaken. She could feel the threads of time weaving through her, an unspoken connection to the very fabric of the universe. The countdown of the candles resonated with her, synchronizing with the pulse of her newfound temporal prowess.

With each passing moment, Olivia's understanding of time deepened. She could glimpse into the recesses of history, witness the unfolding present, and catch fleeting glimpses of potential futures. The unspoken ties between her and the candles unfolded like a cosmic ballet, each movement revealing the intricate choreography of temporal manipulation.

The sanctum of Montgomery Clockworks became a crucible of cosmic energies, and Olivia Bennett stood at its center, a conduit for the unfolding events. The candles, guardians of time's secrets, recognized in her a kindred spirit—a custodian of the temporal wonders that danced within the space-time ripples. The cosmic countdown continued, and Olivia, bound by unspoken ties, embraced her role in the unfolding tapestry of Eldritch Yule.

Amidst the spectral glow of the candles and the temporal anomalies that ebbed and flowed, Professor Reginald Montgomery delved into the arcane knowledge he held as the custodian of Montgomery Clockworks. With each passing moment of the cosmic countdown, he unraveled deeper insights into the forces that governed time itself.

The ancient timepieces within the clockworks manifested as the candles held secrets that transcended the ordinary understanding of temporal mechanics. With a lifetime devoted to studying these cosmic wonders, Professor Montgomery deciphered the intricacies of the celestial ballet playing out before him.

Temporal insights unfolded like pages of an otherworldly tome. The professor revealed the interconnected dance of past, present, and future—a tapestry woven with threads of cosmic energies. He spoke of the ephemeral flames as conduits to realms unseen, where the boundaries of time blurred and the mysteries of the universe whispered in the language of celestial secrets.

As Professor Montgomery shared his revelations, Olivia Bennett listened intently, her connection to the candles amplifying her grasp of the temporal intricacies. The clockwork sanctum resonated with the wisdom of ages. Amid the cosmic revelations, the candles continued their countdown, marking the passage of time and unraveling the enigmatic tale of Eldritch Yule.

As the candles' countdown progressed, the chronological flux intensified, creating ripples in the very fabric of time. Temporal anomalies expanded, challenging the boundaries of reality and perception in ways that defied the conventional understanding of the world.

Glimpses into the past, present, and future merged, creating a kaleidoscope of events that unfolded simultaneously. The temporal unraveling brought forth echoes of bygone eras, snippets of possible futures, and moments frozen in the present, all intermingling in a cosmic dance.

Within the clockwork sanctum, Professor Montgomery and Olivia Bennett found themselves navigating the ever-shifting currents of time. The once-stable reality became a fluid tapestry, where cause and effect lost their linear constraints. The consequences of the candles' countdown were felt not just within the confines of the clockworks. Still, they reverberated outward, touching the very essence of Eldritch Yule.

The villagers, unaware of the cosmic intricacies at play, experienced the effects of the temporal flux. Familiar landscapes transformed, relationships underwent profound shifts, and the quaint town became a nexus of temporal possibilities. The consequences of each fleeting moment echoed through the ages, leaving an indelible mark on the cosmic canvas.

The chronological flux deepened as the candles continued their countdown, weaving a tale of temporal unpredictability and cosmic uncertainty. The unraveling of time became both a challenge and an opportunity—an exploration of the unknown realms that lay beyond the conventional boundaries of existence.

As the candles' countdown reached its zenith, a profound stillness settled over Montgomery Clockworks. The temporal turbulence that had gripped the sanctum eased into a moment of eerie tranquility. The spectral glow from the candles, once flickering with temporal uncertainty, now radiated a steady brilliance, casting a warm and ethereal light throughout the clockwork haven.

The chronological flux that had woven a tapestry of temporal anomalies began to subside, and the once-shifting reality found a moment of equilibrium. The consequences of the candles' cosmic countdown became anchored in a temporal stabilization, freezing past, present, and future echoes into a harmonious coexistence.

Professor Reginald Montgomery and Olivia Bennett felt the palpable shift in the cosmic currents within the sanctum. Once conduits of temporal chaos, the candles now stood as beacons of a stabilized reality. The mysteries of the candles, their ancient properties, and their enigmatic countdown became etched into the very essence of Montgomery Clockworks.

As the spectral glow lingered, casting a celestial aura over the intricate timepieces and ancient mechanisms, the clockwork haven bore witness to the culmination of the cosmic events. The once unpredictable dance of time had found a moment of respite, leaving behind a legacy that transcended the ordinary boundaries of existence.

Montgomery Clockworks, forever marked by time candles, was a testament to the cosmic forces gracing Eldritch Yule. The temporal stabilization became a defining moment in the town's history, a reminder of the intricate dance between cosmic energies and the fabric of time itself. The villagers, unaware of the celestial ballet within the clockwork sanctum, continued their festivities, forever changed by the unseen forces that had woven their influence into the very fabric of Eldritch Yule.

Amid the festive warmth of the Thompson Residence, the hearth crackled with a comforting glow, casting a dance of shadows on the walls adorned with holiday decorations. The air was filled with the scent of freshly baked treats, and the family gathered around the festive hearth, their eyes gleaming with the anticipation of what the stockings might hold.

As the family exchanged heartfelt gifts, the stockings hung by the fireplace took on a special significance. Each member of the Thompson family had a stocking adorned with care, patiently waiting to be unveiled. Little did they know that a celestial secret lay within the cozy confines of these festive stockings. This otherworldly surprise would weave a cosmic thread into their Christmas celebration.

Unbeknownst to the family, the stockings harbored portals to celestial realms. A subtle shimmer danced along the edges of the stockings, hinting at the ethereal journey awaiting those who dared to peer inside. The celestial realm portals, concealed within the fabric of the stockings, held the promise of a cosmic adventure, intertwining the mundane with the extraordinary.

As the family continued to revel in the joyous festivities, the celestial realm portals beckoned, their cosmic energies pulsating in tandem with the beat of the holiday spirit. The hearth, aglow with the warmth of familial love, became a focal point for the celestial and terrestrial convergence—a threshold between the ordinary and the extraordinary.

Little did the Thompsons suspect the cosmic surprises concealed within the stockings, nor could they fathom the celestial realms that awaited them. As the last embers of the festive hearth glowed, the family stood on the brink of a stellar journey, their stockings poised to unravel the celestial wonders that would redefine the boundaries of their Christmas celebration.

In the heart of the Thompson Residence, Sarah filled with the enchantment of Christmas traditions, gazed eagerly at the festive stockings. Little did she suspect the celestial journey that awaited her within the folds of the shimmering fabric. Beside her stood Samuel, her companion, blissfully unaware of the cosmic events about to unfold through the stellar stockings.

As the family continued their holiday festivities, Sarah and Samuel approached the hearth, drawn by the allure of the stockings hanging by the fireplace. Sarah's eyes sparkled with the wonder of a child, and she couldn't resist the urge to peek inside the stocking bearing her name. With a gentle touch, she unfurled the celestial portal concealed within.

A soft glow emanated from the depths of the stocking, enveloping Sarah and Samuel in a celestial aura. The mundane surroundings of the Thompson Residence began to fade, replaced by the surreal landscapes of a celestial realm. The hearth transformed into a cosmic gateway, and the stockings, once ordinary, now pulsed with otherworldly energies.

Sarah and Samuel were transported to a realm where the stars painted the sky in hues unseen on Earth. Celestial beings moved gracefully, and the air carried the whispers of cosmic secrets. The stellar stockings had become conduits to a dimension beyond imagination, and the Thompsons were now spectators in a celestial spectacle.

Unaware of the cosmic forces, Sarah and Samuel marveled at the ethereal wonders surrounding them. The stockings, now imbued with celestial magic, became tokens of their journey—a reminder that the boundaries between the ordinary and the cosmic were as thin as the fabric of the stockings themselves.

As the Thompsons navigated the celestial realm, the hearth in their earthly abode continued to burn with festive warmth. Unbeknownst to the family, the stockings hung by the fireplace had become portals to a stellar adventure, forever altering the course of their Christmas celebration.

In the heart of the Thompson Residence, a cozy Christmas ambiance enveloped the air, creating a warm haven for holiday celebrations. The crackling hearth cast a gentle glow across the room, illuminating the festive decorations adorning the walls. Stockings, carefully hung by the fireplace, dangled in anticipation of surprises hidden within their folds.

The Thompson family gathered in the living room, immersed in the joyous spirit of the season. The scent of freshly baked cookies wafted through the air, and the twinkling lights of the Christmas tree added to the festive glow. Laughter echoed as family members shared stories, exchanged gifts, and reveled in the simple pleasures of togetherness.

The hearth, with its flickering flames, became the room's focal point—a source of both physical warmth and emotional comfort. Adorned with care, the stockings waited patiently to be explored, each a vessel of potential wonders.

As the family embraced the coziness of their Christmas haven, little did they know that within the stockings lay not only traditional surprises but also celestial portals to realms beyond imagination. The cosmic journey hidden within the folds of fabric was a secret yet to be unveiled, a magical twist to their familiar holiday traditions. The Thompson Residence, aglow with festive cheer, witnessed the intertwining of the ordinary and the cosmic, where each stocking held the promise of a stellar adventure.

With a childlike enthusiasm, Sarah eagerly embraced the time-honored Christmas traditions that made the holiday season truly magical. Among these traditions, her love for stockings and anticipating their surprises stood out as a beacon of joy. In the Thompson Residence, the stockings weren't just festive accessories; they were vessels of enchantment, holding the promise of wondrous discoveries.

With each year, Sarah's excitement for the stockings grew. She reveled in the tradition of hanging them by the fireplace, a visual representation of the warmth and togetherness that the season brought. Filling the stockings with small surprises became a cherished ritual to express love and appreciation for the family's unique bonds.

Little did Sarah know that this Christmas would bring a cosmic twist to her beloved tradition. Usually filled with delightful and mundane surprises, the stockings now harbored celestial portals, opening doorways to realms beyond the ordinary. As she gazed at the stockings with a twinkle in her eye, Sarah was unknowingly on the brink of a cosmic journey that would redefine the meaning of holiday magic. Once symbols of festive joy, the stellar stockings were about to become conduits to an otherworldly adventure that awaited the unsuspecting Thompson family.

As Sarah approached the stockings with gleeful anticipation, little did she suspect the extraordinary transformation awaiting the seemingly ordinary fabric vessels. The mantelpiece, adorned with festive decorations and the glow of holiday lights, held the innocent surprises that would soon transcend the boundaries of the mundane.

As she reached for the stockings, a subtle energy permeated the air, invisible to the naked eye but charged with cosmic significance. The fabric, once merely a vessel for small gifts and treats, now pulsed with an otherworldly essence. With a childlike curiosity, Sarah tugged at the stockings, unleashing a cascade of cosmic wonders.

In a shimmering display, the fabric of the stockings rippled like the surface of a celestial pond, and portals to distant realms unfolded before Sarah's astonished eyes. The innocent surprises she had expected were replaced by cosmic landscapes, each stocking unveiling a portal to a celestial realm beyond human imagination.

The air tingled with the scent of cosmic energies as the ordinary living room transformed into a gateway to the unknown. The innocent tradition of exploring the contents of the stockings now became a cosmic journey. With wide eyes and a heart full of wonder, Sarah stepped into the stellar portals, ready to explore the celestial wonders that awaited her on this enchanted Christmas night.

In the cozy glow of the Thompson Residence, Samuel's attention was captivated by the radiant allure of the stellar stockings. Intrigued by the cosmic energy that seemed to dance around them, he couldn't resist the urge to explore the unexpected discovery concealed within the fabric vessels.

The air around him seemed to hum with an otherworldly resonance as he approached the stockings, drawing him closer to the celestial realm portals hidden within the seemingly ordinary Christmas tradition. With a mixture of curiosity and wonder, Samuel reached out. He touched the fabric, feeling a subtle vibration beneath his fingertips.

To his amazement, the stockings responded to his touch, unfurling like ancient scrolls to reveal portals that shimmered with cosmic radiance. Once familiar and comforting, the room now transformed into a gateway to realms beyond the stars. Samuel, unknowingly opening the gateway to cosmic wonders, hesitated for a moment before stepping into the unknown.

As he crossed the threshold of the celestial realm portals, the cozy ambiance of the Thompson Residence gave way to ethereal landscapes, where constellations twinkled in hues unseen by mortal eyes. Samuel was immersed in a cosmic tapestry, an unwitting traveler in a realm where the ordinary merged seamlessly with the extraordinary. The unexpected discovery within the stellar stockings had opened a doorway to a celestial journey that would forever alter the course of this enchanting Eldritch Yule night.

Within the celestial realms unveiled by the stellar stockings, Samuel was surrounded by otherworldly landscapes that transcended the limits of earthly imagination. The air shimmered with the essence of cosmic wonders, and ethereal landscapes stretched before him like an uncharted tapestry.

Strange constellations adorned the skies, forming patterns that whispered ancient tales of celestial beings and cosmic forces. Samuel walked upon grounds that seemed to shift between solid reality and intangible dreams, where the laws of nature bent to the will of cosmic entities that lingered in the celestial expanse.

Mountains made of crystalline stardust loomed in the distance, their peaks reaching toward astral heavens that pulsed with vibrant hues unseen by mortal eyes. Rivers of liquid light flowed through the surreal landscapes, carrying with them the energies of distant galaxies and the mysteries of the cosmos.

As Samuel journeyed further into the celestial realms, he encountered entities of cosmic splendor—beings whose forms defied earthly comprehension. Some were ephemeral wisps of starlight, while others took on majestic forms reminiscent of celestial deities. They observed Samuel with eyes that held the wisdom of eons, acknowledging his presence in their cosmic domain.

The stellar stockings, once innocent vessels of Christmas tradition, had become gateways to a realm where the boundaries between the mundane and the cosmic blurred into an awe-inspiring tapestry of celestial wonders. Samuel, a humble participant in this cosmic journey, marveled at the breathtaking beauty and enigmatic nature of the ethereal landscapes that unfolded before him. Little did he know that the celestial realms held secrets and revelations that would forever intertwine his destiny with the cosmic forces on this mystical Eldritch Yule night.

Guided by the enchantment concealed within the stellar stockings, Sarah stepped into a cosmic adventure that transcended the boundaries of the familiar. As she passed through the celestial portal, the hearth's cozy warmth gave way to an otherworldly radiance, and she emerged in a realm where the very fabric of reality seemed to dance with ethereal energies.

Celestial beings, radiant and otherworldly, greeted Sarah with a graceful acknowledgment. Their luminous forms pulsed with the essence of cosmic forces, and their eyes held the wisdom of ages untold. Sarah was filled with wonder, journeying alongside these celestial entities through landscapes that defied earthly description.

Ethereal meadows adorned with blooms that emitted the soft glow of distant stars stretched out in all directions. The air was alive with harmonious melodies, a celestial symphony composed by unseen cosmic hands. Sarah's footsteps echoed through crystalline pathways wound through the surreal expanse, each step revealing new wonders.

As Sarah ventured deeper into the celestial realms, she encountered celestial gardens where flora of cosmic origin flourished. Blossoms emitted hues unseen by mortal eyes, and their petals seemed to capture the essence of nebulae and galaxies. The celestial beings guided Sarah through these gardens, sharing the secrets of the surrounding cosmic tapestry.

The stellar stockings, once mere fabric vessels hanging by the fireplace, had become portals to a celestial adventure that unfolded with each step Sarah took. The journey through the realms beyond the ordinary became a testament to the boundless wonders hidden within the cosmic embrace of Eldritch Yule. Little did Sarah know that her celestial odyssey held revelations that would forever alter her perception of the universe, intertwining her fate with the cosmic forces that graced this magical night.

Samuel, lured by the allure of the stellar stockings and the ethereal glow emanating from the celestial portal, found himself unwittingly swept into the cosmic current alongside Sarah. As he passed through the stocking portal, the familiar hearthside glow dissolved into the luminous radiance of the celestial realms.

Sarah and Samuel, now cosmic companions, discovered landscapes that defied earthly comprehension. The celestial beings, their forms aglow with cosmic energies, welcomed Samuel into their midst with an otherworldly grace. The duo journeyed together through meadows adorned with blooms that radiated the brilliance of distant stars, the echoes of celestial melodies guiding their way.

Ethereal gardens unfolded before them, where flora of cosmic origin flourished in vibrant hues. The celestial entities shared the secrets of the cosmic tapestry, revealing the interconnected threads that wove through the fabric of reality. Samuel, filled with awe, followed Sarah through crystalline pathways, each step revealing new wonders that surpassed the limits of mortal imagination.

As companions in this accidental cosmic journey, Sarah and Samuel faced challenges and marveled at celestial wonders that tested the boundaries of their understanding. The celestial realms, once hidden within the innocent guise of Christmas stockings, now became a playground for the duo's exploration and discovery.

Amid these cosmic landscapes, where time seemed to dance to an unearthly rhythm, Sarah and Samuel's connection deepened. They became witnesses to the celestial ballet, where the interplay of cosmic forces painted a tableau that transcended the ordinary. Little did they know that their accidental venture into the celestial realms would leave an indelible mark on their souls, forever entwining their fates with the mysteries of Eldritch Yule.

Amidst the celestial wonders, Sarah and Samuel engaged in joyous encounters with the ethereal beings that populated the cosmic realms. The celestial entities' luminous forms pulsating with cosmic energy extended warm greetings to the accidental travelers.

In this otherworldly tapestry, the cosmic inhabitants embraced the duo, inviting them to join in celestial celebrations that echoed with melodies unheard by mortal ears. The joyous encounters unfolded like a cosmic dance, where Sarah and Samuel became integral participants in the celestial revelry.

Radiant beings with wings adorned in starlight twirled alongside them, and ethereal music filled the cosmic air, resonating with the familiar tunes of festive carols. The celestial entities, with faces aglow like constellations, exchanged expressions of joy and merriment with their newfound companions.

As Sarah and Samuel navigated the cosmic landscapes, they discovered that the stellar stockings served as portals and conduits for the blending of Christmas magic and cosmic wonders. The joyous encounters became a harmonious fusion of earthly traditions and celestial festivities, creating a celebration that transcended the boundaries of both realms.

Sarah and Samuel forged connections with the cosmic entities that would leave a lasting imprint on their hearts through laughter, shared moments, and celestial dances. In the cosmic embrace of the celestial beings, the accidental travelers found a sense of belonging, realizing that the magic of Eldritch Yule extended far beyond the hearthside warmth of their earthly home.

Sarah and Samuel delved into the heart of cosmic mysteries within the celestial realms accessed through the stellar stockings. The landscapes transformed, shifting from ethereal wonders to realms adorned with constellations that mirrored the starry patterns of the winter night sky.

As they traversed these cosmic landscapes, revelations unfolded like petals of an otherworldly flower. Celestial beings guided them through realms where time flowed differently, and the boundaries between past, present, and future blurred in a harmonious dance. Through the stellar portals, the mysteries of the cosmos intertwined with the festive hearth, creating a cosmic tapestry that resonated with the wonders of Eldritch Yule.

The celestial entities shared tales of ancient cosmic events, where the celestial and earthly realms converged during the magical nights of Eldritch Yule. Sarah and Samuel, enchanted by these revelations, discovered that the festive traditions they held dear were intricately linked to cosmic forces that transcended their understanding.

Within the portals, they witnessed the cosmic origins of familiar Yuletide symbols—the celestial inspiration behind snowflakes, the cosmic dance that inspired holiday lights, and the echoes of ancient cosmic beings in the laughter of celestial children.

As the cosmic secrets unfolded, Sarah and Samuel felt a profound connection between the hearthside warmth of their earthly home and the celestial wonders that embraced them in the cosmic realms. The revelations within the portals became threads woven into the fabric of their understanding, connecting the mundane and the cosmic in a tapestry of Eldritch Yule magic.

The cosmic journey through the stellar stockings came to a close as Sarah and Samuel emerged from the celestial realms, their eyes readjusting to the familiar surroundings of the Thompson Residence. The hearth, adorned with stockings and the remnants of Christmas festivities, welcomed them back with the comforting warmth of home.

As they stepped out of the cosmic portals, the ethereal landscapes dissipated like morning mist, leaving only the residual glow of cosmic magic lingering in the air. The celestial beings bid farewell with smiles that echoed starlight as the stellar stockings reverted to their ordinary, mundane appearance.

Yet, despite the return to the earthly realm, Sarah and Samuel felt a subtle shift in the atmosphere—a connection forged between the festive hearth and the cosmic wonders they had encountered. The knowledge gained within the celestial realms became a cherished part of their holiday traditions, transforming the ordinary into something extraordinary.

Once a symbol of warmth and familial joy, the hearth now held the whispers of cosmic secrets, and the stockings, once superficial vessels for surprises, became conduits between the mundane and the celestial. The celestial bridge they had crossed left an indelible mark on the Thompson Residence, forever intertwining the magic of Christmas with the cosmic unknown.

As they settled back into the familiar comforts of their home, Sarah and Samuel carried with them the cosmic revelations of the stellar stockings—a gift from the celestial realms that would continue to echo through the remaining nights of Eldritch Yule, turning the ordinary into the extraordinary with each passing moment.

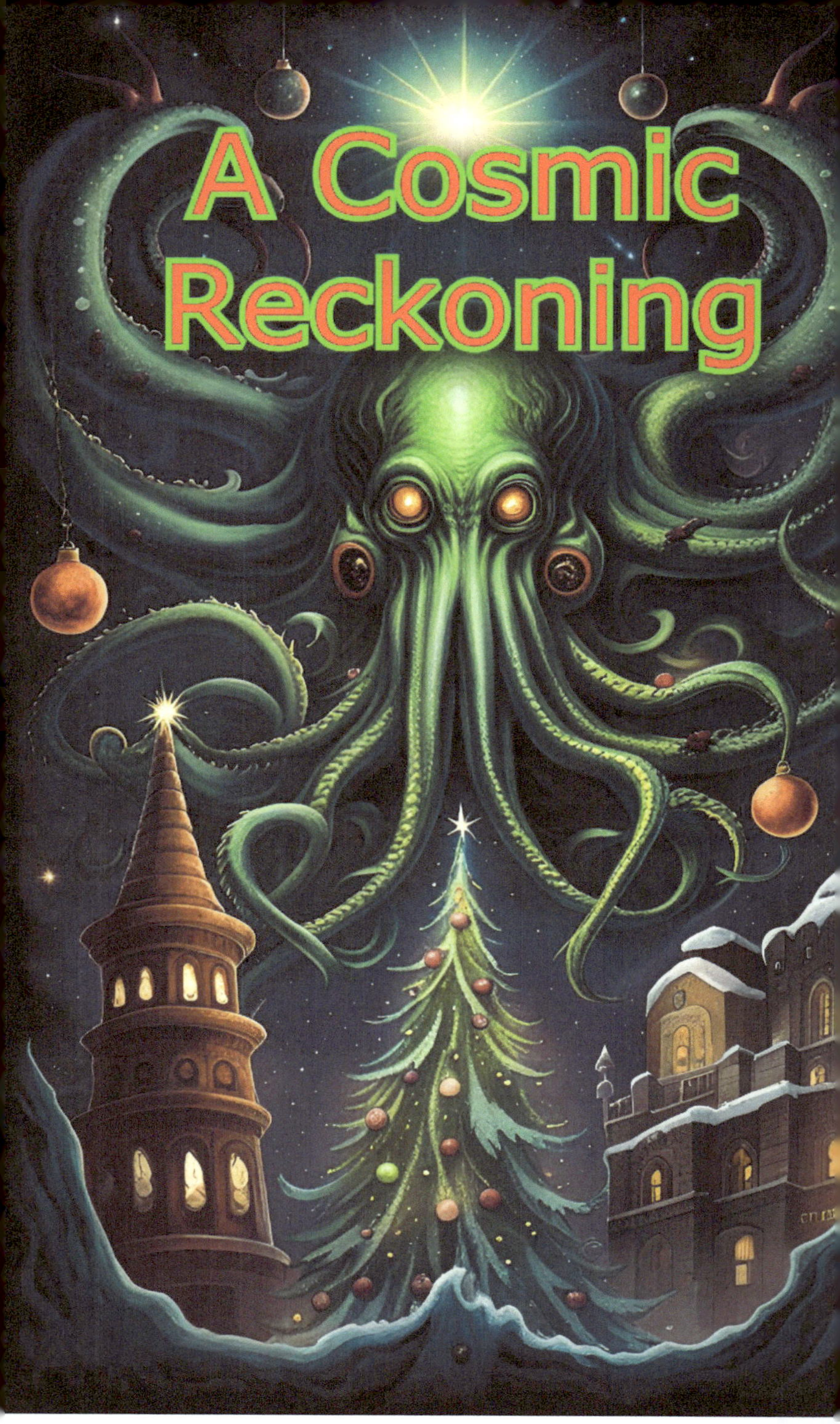

A Cosmic Reckoning

In the ethereal confines of the Library Nexus, cosmic energies pulsed like the universe's heartbeat. It was a convergence point where the threads of the tales woven across Eldritch Yule intertwined, creating a cosmic tapestry that whispered of eldritch mysteries and impending reckoning.

Within the cosmic nexus, fragments of the Nutcracker's astral ballet lingered, entwined with the crimson snowfall's temporal echoes and the ephemeral mistletoe's emotional resonances. The stellar stockings' celestial wonders hovered in the air, creating an intricate dance of cosmic forces. The candles of time, their enigmatic countdown complete, cast shadows that whispered of temporal flux.

Amidst the shelves of cosmic knowledge, Professor Reginald Montgomery, Dr. Isabella Hartfield, Clara Bellamy, Elizabeth Montgomery, Sarah Thompson, and other unwitting protagonists were drawn to the cosmic nexus. This convergence transcended the boundaries of their individual stories.

The cosmic energies surged as the clock struck midnight, forming a vortex at the Convergence Point. Eldritch entities began to manifest, born from the fusion of astral ballet, crimson snowfall, ephemeral mistletoe, stellar stockings, and candles of time. Beyond the comprehension of mortal minds, these eldritch beings stirred in the cosmic cauldron, ready to enact a reckoning that would reshape the fabric of reality.

The protagonists, guided by the cosmic forces intertwined in their tales, stood at the threshold of the midnight reckoning. Each carried the essence of their cosmic encounters—Clara's astral ballet connection, Dr. Hartfield's meteorological insights, Elizabeth's mistletoe-induced journey, and Sarah and Samuel's celestial voyage.

The Library Nexus hummed with cosmic anticipation, and as the eldritch entities prepared to step into the earthly realm, the protagonists braced themselves for a cosmic reckoning that would decide the fate of Eldritch Yule and the intertwined destinies of those caught in the cosmic web.

Midnight approached, and the Library Nexus became the epicenter of a cosmic storm—a swirling dance of eldritch energies heralding the climax of the intertwined tales. The protagonists, united by the cosmic threads that bound them, stood firm as the cosmic reckoning unfolded, embracing the unknown that awaited them at the Convergence Point.

Dr. Evelyn Blackthorn, surrounded by ancient tomes and the weight of cosmic knowledge, delved deeper into the Canticles of Yule. The cryptic verses unfolded a tale of Eldritch's prophecy. This cosmic weave transcended time and space, revealing a path that intertwined with the unfolding tales of Eldritch Yule.

In her quest for understanding, Dr. Blackthorn was guided by the enigmatic Professor Nathaniel Eldritch. A figure shrouded in cosmic mysteries, Eldritch unraveled the secrets concealed within the Canticles, unveiling the connection between the astral ballet, crimson snowfall, ephemeral mistletoe, stellar stockings, candles of time, and the impending midnight reckoning at the Convergence Point.

The Canticles foretold the arrival of the Eldritch Council, cosmic beings beyond mortal comprehension, who governed the eldritch forces woven into the fabric of the universe. As midnight drew near, Dr. Blackthorn sensed the convergence of cosmic energies, heralding the manifestation of the Eldritch Council at the Convergence Point.

In the Library Nexus, where the tales of Eldritch Yule converged, Dr. Blackthorn prepared to face the consequences of unlocking the eldritch prophecy. The Canticles had become a double-edged tome, offering enlightenment and peril in equal measure. With each verse deciphered, the cosmic tapestry tightened its grip on the destinies within its threads.

At the stroke of midnight, the Eldritch Council materialized—a surreal presence that defied mortal understanding. Cosmic energies crackled around them as they observed the protagonists, their forms flickering with the essence of astral ballet, crimson snowfall, mistletoe, celestial realms, and the inexorable march of time.

In the presence of the Eldritch Council, Dr. Blackthorn felt the weight of her discoveries. The cosmic tales had converged, and the midnight reckoning had begun. The protagonists, unwittingly connected by the cosmic forces, stood at the nexus of destinies, awaiting the outcome of a cosmic dance that would determine the course of Eldritch Yule and the fates entangled within its eldritch embrace.

The Library Nexus shimmered with an otherworldly glow, its shelves adorned with tomes that held the weight of cosmic secrets. Dr. Evelyn Blackthorn, Professor Nathaniel Eldritch, Clara from the astral ballet, Major General Drummond from the crimson snowfall, Elizabeth and Thomas touched by the ephemeral mistletoe, Sarah and Samuel with celestial realms in their stockings, and the custodian of time, Professor Reginald Montgomery—all stood within this astral repository.

The air crackled with the anticipation of cosmic revelation as the protagonists, unwittingly connected by the eldritch tapestry, gathered to confront the impending manifestation of the Eldritch Council. The

Canticles of Yule, decoded by Dr. Blackthorn, echoed through the ethereal halls, guiding and warning for the cosmic dance that awaited them.

Each protagonist, a living embodiment of one facet of Eldritch Yule, shared a moment of recognition—a cosmic acknowledgment that their individual tales were threads woven into the grand tapestry of cosmic events. The astral ballet, crimson snowfall, ephemeral mistletoe, stellar stockings, and time candles converge at this nexus of knowledge and destiny.

The Eldritch Council, enigmatic cosmic beings, watched from the fringes of reality as the protagonists prepared to face the consequences of their unwitting participation in the eldritch prophecy. The astral repository held the answers to the questions that had haunted them throughout the cosmic tales—questions of purpose, destiny, and the cosmic forces that bound them together.

The protagonists steeled themselves for the impending midnight reckoning in this celestial library. The Canticles whispered truths and warnings, and the Eldritch Council, with their astral forms pulsating with cosmic energy, observed the convergence of destinies. The Library Nexus, a threshold between mortal understanding and eldritch knowledge, became the stage for the cosmic dance that would determine the fate of Eldritch Yule and the protagonists forever changed by its eldritch embrace.

As Dr. Evelyn Blackthorn recounted her journey, the astral repository pulsated with the resonance of the Canticles of Yule. This journey began with the innocent pursuit of knowledge and led her to the cosmic tapestry woven throughout Eldritch Yule.

From deciphering the ancient verses to unlocking the secrets hidden within the eldritch verses, Dr. Blackthorn's odyssey served as the catalyst for the intertwining tales of the astral ballet, crimson snowfall, ephemeral mistletoe, stellar stockings, and the candles of time. Her discoveries, a symphony of eldritch truths, echoed through the astral repository, linking each protagonist to the impending cosmic reckoning.

The Nutcracker's cosmic ballet, Major General Drummond's revelation in the crimson snow, Clara's astral connection, Dr. Isabella Hartfield's meteorological marvels, Johnathan Whitman's unwitting role, Elizabeth Montgomery's ephemeral mistletoe experience, the temporal anomalies witnessed by Professor Reginald Montgomery, the celestial realms within the stockings explored by Sarah and Samuel—all found their origin in the Canticles of Yule.

As Dr. Blackthorn spoke, the protagonists absorbed the weight of their roles in the cosmic drama. The interconnectedness of their experiences became apparent, each tale a piece of the larger puzzle that led them to this moment—the eve of the midnight reckoning.

The Eldritch Council observed as the culmination of discoveries reverberated through the Library Nexus. The cosmic threads that bound the tales of the protagonists together into a singular story of Eldritch Yule were entwined with the eldritch prophecy. Destiny awaited its reckoning, all witnessed by the spectral Council.

As Dr. Evelyn Blackthorn continued to share her revelations in the astral repository, the focus shifted to her mysterious mentor, Professor Nathaniel Eldritch. The ethereal glow of the Canticles of Yule played upon his enigmatic countenance, casting shadows that danced with the eldritch energies surrounding him.

Professor Eldritch, a sage of cosmic wisdom, stood as a guiding force in Dr. Blackthorn's journey. His eyes held the weight of eons, and his voice resonated with the echoes of eldritch truths. As the celestial repository embraced their presence, he unveiled the layers of his knowledge, each piece a fragment of the cosmic puzzle.

His connection to the eldritch entities became evident, woven into the fabric of the Canticles and transcending the boundaries of mortal understanding. The mysterious mentor's role was not merely academic; it was a cosmic dance, a choreography of guidance leading Dr. Blackthorn through the cosmic mysteries embedded within the verses.

Professor Eldritch's revelations echoed through the astral repository, creating a harmonious convergence of knowledge and destiny. As the protagonists absorbed the essence of his teachings, the eldritch entities, silent witnesses to the unfolding cosmic drama, stirred with anticipation at the threshold of the midnight reckoning.

The astral repository became a nexus of understanding, where the mentor's cosmic insights merged with the discoveries of Dr. Blackthorn and the interconnected tales of Eldritch Yule. The Canticles, once cryptic verses, now unfolded as a cosmic map guiding them toward the impending convergence point. This midnight reckoning would mark the culmination of cosmic destinies.

The air became charged with anticipation at the Convergence Point, where the astral repository and the cosmic energies intertwined. The veil between realms shimmered as The Eldritch Council manifested, their cosmic presence transcending mortal comprehension.

The Eldritch Council, enigmatic cosmic beings, materialized in a celestial symphony of radiant energy. Each member embodied a facet of the eldritch forces—ancient, inscrutable entities governing the cosmic dance. Their forms, ever-shifting and adorned with cosmic constellations, exuded an otherworldly aura that rippled through the astral repository.

As the luminous figures of The Eldritch Council took their positions, the midnight reckoning drew near. The Canticles of Yule resonated with cosmic echoes, and the protagonists, gathered in awe, felt the weight of the impending cosmic revelation.

The Council's arrival marked the convergence of destinies, the culmination of the interconnected tales woven through the cosmic threads of Eldritch Yule. The astral repository, a sacred space where knowledge and cosmic energies coalesced, became the stage for the cosmic manifestation.

The Eldritch Council, with eyes, mirrored the cosmos, surveyed the protagonists with a knowing gaze. Their presence signaled the end of a cosmic journey and the beginning of a new phase in the eternal dance of eldritch forces.

The astral repository pulsed with cosmic energies as the midnight reckoning loomed, and the Canticles of Yule reached a crescendo. The Convergence Point stood as the nexus where mortal and cosmic destinies converged, setting the stage for the revelations that would shape the very fabric of reality.

At the Library Nexus, the protagonists from disparate tales were drawn together, their individual destinies converging like threads in the cosmic tapestry of Eldritch Yule. The astral repository became a meeting ground for those who had navigated the eldritch mysteries, each carrying the weight of their experiences and revelations.

Sarah, Samuel, Clara, Dr. Hartfield, Elizabeth, Thomas, Olivia, and others—all stood at the epicenter of a cosmic convergence. The interwoven fates of these individuals mirrored the complex dance of celestial bodies, guided by forces beyond mortal understanding.

The Canticles of Yule, discovered by Dr. Evelyn Blackthorn, resonated with cosmic echoes, echoing the interconnectedness of their stories. The Library Nexus, a haven of cosmic knowledge, held the key to understanding the intricate patterns that bound their fates together.

As The Eldritch Council observed, their cosmic gaze acknowledged each protagonist's roles in the grand tapestry of Eldritch Yule. The astral repository pulsed with energy, responding to the convergence of destinies, and the protagonists, bound by unseen forces, prepared for the midnight reckoning that would shape the course of their existence.

In this celestial gathering, the intertwining fates of the protagonists served as a testament to the lasting impact of cosmic phenomena. These individual stories merged to create a collective saga that unfolded under the cosmic scrutiny of The Eldritch Council. The Library Nexus, bathed in the mystical radiance of cosmic knowledge, bore witness to this cosmic reunion where destinies collided and the true essence of Eldritch Yule began to reveal itself.

As the protagonists stood within the Library Nexus, the Canticles of Yule, discovered by Dr. Evelyn Blackthorn, began to resonate with otherworldly energy. The astral repository pulsated with cosmic vibrations, and the Canticles unfurled like ancient scrolls, unveiling the eldritch prophecy that had remained shrouded in cosmic mystery.

Words written in ethereal ink glowed upon the astral pages, and the celestial language of the Canticles whispered truths that transcended time and space. The eldritch prophecy, intricately woven into the fabric of the cosmos, was now laid bare before those who had become unwitting participants in its cosmic dance.

The Canticles spoke of cosmic energies converging during the sacred 12 Nights of Eldritch Yule, where the mundane and cosmic boundaries would thin. It foretold interwoven destinies, celestial realms, and the manifestation of eldritch entities drawn to the tapestry of Christmas celebrations.

As the Canticles of Yule unfurled, the protagonists, linked by the threads of fate, absorbed the cosmic revelations etched in the astral pages. Long veiled in mystery, the eldritch destiny now stood before them, a roadmap to the midnight reckoning that would mark the culmination of their cosmic journey.

The Library Nexus echoed with the resonant power of the Canticles, and the protagonists, their eyes alight with newfound understanding, prepared to face the cosmic forces unleashed during the 12 Nights of Eldritch Yule. The Eldritch Prophecy, now unveiled, became a guiding light in the celestial darkness, steering them towards the cosmic climax that awaited at the Convergence Point.

The Library Nexus quivered with an astral resonance, a cosmic tug-of-war unfolding among the protagonists, the eldritch entities, and The Eldritch Council. Threads of fate intertwined, and the very fabric of reality seemed to shimmer with the impending clash of cosmic forces.

Fueled by the revelations of the Canticles of Yule, the protagonists stood resolute, their spirits aligned with the eldritch destiny foretold in the celestial prophecy. Dr. Evelyn Blackthorn, guided by the cosmic knowledge bestowed by Professor Nathaniel Eldritch, took the forefront, a beacon of determination in the face of the astral turmoil.

On the opposing side, eldritch entities were drawn from various tales about the 12 Nights of Eldritch Yule. These entities were visible as ethereal beings, with each embodiment representing a grotesque manifestation of cosmic malevolence. Their power crackled in the astral space as they aimed to gain control over the unfolding events.

Above them all loomed The Eldritch Council, enigmatic cosmic beings with unfathomable wisdom. Their presence was both a stabilizing force and an arbiter of the cosmic balance, observing the astral tug-of-war with a detached yet vested interest in the outcome.

The astral tug-of-war intensified as the protagonists, guided by the Canticles, invoked cosmic energies to counter the eldritch entities' bid for supremacy. The Library Nexus, caught in the maelstrom of cosmic forces, became a battleground where fate and free will collided in a celestial clash.

The essence of the 12 Nights of Eldritch Yule hung in the balance, a cosmic struggle that would determine the destiny of the protagonists and the eldritch entities. As the midnight reckoning neared, the astral tug-of-war reached its zenith, and the Library Nexus became the epicenter of a cosmic confrontation that would echo through the realms beyond the ordinary.

The Library Nexus quivered as the eldritch entities materialized, their cosmic forms intertwining with the protagonists' realities. Ethereal tendrils of eldritch energy extended from their otherworldly presence, reaching into the very essence of the astral space.

Dr. Evelyn Blackthorn, flanked by those whose fates had become intricately entwined during the 12 Nights of Eldritch Yule, stood defiant in the face of the eldritch manifestation. The air crackled with a surreal tension as the protagonists confronted the eldritch entities, the astral battleground now charged with the cosmic energies of destiny.

The eldritch entities, embodying cosmic malevolence, shifted and undulated in forms that transcended mortal comprehension. Their presence exuded an otherworldly malevolence that seeped into the fabric of reality, warping the very nature of the Library Nexus.

The astral tug-of-war reached its zenith, and the protagonists, fueled by the revelations of the Canticles of Yule, sought to challenge the eldritch entities' bid for dominance. The clash between destiny and malevolence manifested in a visual spectacle—a cosmic ballet of light and shadows, the dance of existence hanging in the balance.

Above all, The Eldritch Council observed with an inscrutable gaze, their cosmic wisdom weaving the unseen threads of fate. The Library Nexus became the convergence point of the cosmic reckoning. On this battleground, the destinies of those entangled in the eldritch tapestry would be decided.

As the otherworldly presence of the eldritch entities and the determined protagonists collided in the astral space, the Library Nexus quivered with the weight of cosmic forces, the climax of the 12 Nights of

Eldritch Yule unfolding in a dance of celestial energies that defied the boundaries of the known and unknown.

The Convergence Point, bathed in the ethereal glow of cosmic energies, became a battleground where temporal forces clash, challenging the fabric of reality and time. The astral tapestry of the Library Nexus quivered as the eldritch entities and the determined protagonists engaged in a celestial struggle.

Temporal unraveling manifested as ripples in the space-time continuum, distorting the linear progression of events. Glimpses of past, present, and future intertwined in a chaotic dance, blurring the boundaries that tethered each moment to its designated place in the cosmic chronology.

Her gaze fixed on the eldritch entities, Dr. Evelyn Blackthorn sensed the unraveling of time around her. The Canticles of Yule, the cosmic prophecy she had unlocked, resonated with the essence of the temporal discord. The protagonists, united by the threads of fate, navigated the fractured reality, each step a precarious dance between the known and the unknown.

The eldritch entities, their cosmic forms undulating with malevolent energy, sought to exploit the temporal chaos, their influence extending into the past and the future. The battleground echoed the clash of destinies as the protagonists, guided by the revelations within the Canticles, endeavored to restore temporal stability.

The Convergence Point, now a nexus of cosmic forces and temporal anomalies, bore witness to a midnight reckoning that transcended the confines of mortal understanding. The astral repository of knowledge became a crucible where the fate of the intertwined tales hung in precarious balance, and the consequences of unlocking the eldritch prophecy rippled through the very fabric of existence.

As the cosmic forces clashed and the temporal unraveling reached its zenith, a profound stillness settled over the Library Nexus. The astral echoes of the cosmic reckoning gradually faded, leaving an eerie resonance lingering in the ethereal air. The protagonists, bathed in the aftermath of the eldritch events, stood amidst the cosmic remnants, their destinies forever altered by the cosmic tug-of-war.

Dr. Evelyn Blackthorn, her eyes reflecting the weight of the revelations within the Canticles of Yule, surveyed the transformed Library Nexus. The eldritch entities, having manifested and dissipated in the cosmic maelstrom, left a subtle imprint on the tapestry of reality. The astral repository, once a sanctuary of cosmic knowledge, now bore witness to the imprints of a struggle that transcended mortal comprehension.

After the temporal anomalies subsided, the protagonists caught glimpses of the altered threads of fate. Connections forged at the Convergence Point lingered, weaving a fresh story across the cosmic tapestry. The consequences of the eldritch prophecy unfolded in unanticipated ways, resonating through the past, present, and future.

In the aftermath of the cosmic reckoning, the Library Nexus stood as a silent testament to the interwoven fates of those who dared to unveil the mysteries of the 12 Nights of Eldritch Yule. The protagonists, marked by the celestial struggle, carried the echoes of a cosmic journey that transcended the boundaries of time and space.

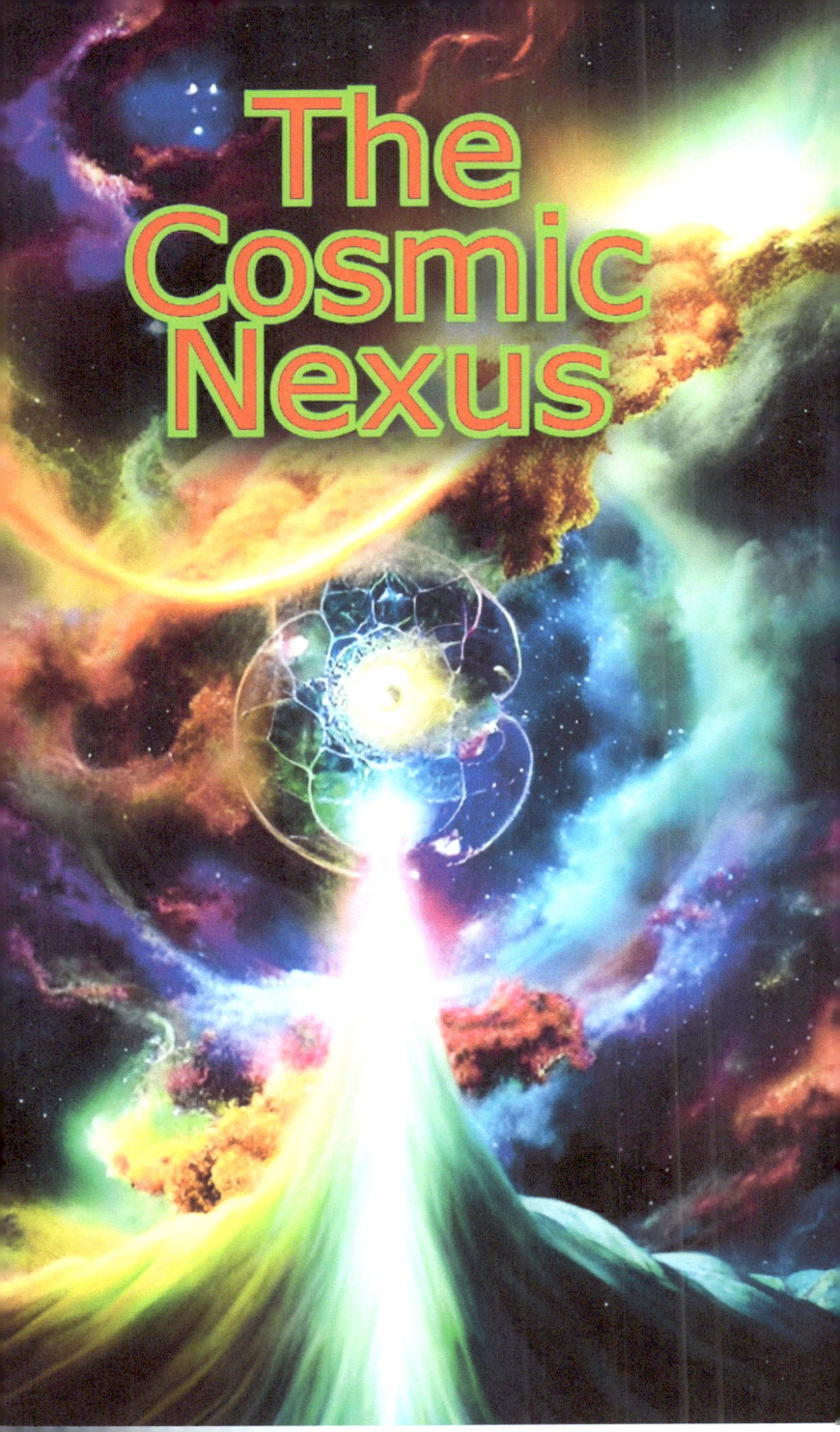

Epilogue

In the ethereal Astral Dominion, where the Eldritch Council held sway over interconnected worlds, a palpable tension lingered in the astral air. Having convened to witness the repercussions of the eldritch events, the cosmic forces awaited the resolution within the sacred Climactic Chamber of the cosmic nexus.

Within the chamber, the astral resonance echoed the cosmic struggle that unfolded in the mortal realm. The Eldritch Council, enigmatic beings of cosmic authority, manifested in forms that transcended mortal comprehension. Their presence resonated with a timeless wisdom, an understanding of the cosmic tapestry woven through the Canticles of Yule.

As the astral entities gathered, the Eldritch Council began unraveling the interwoven threads of destiny during the 12 Nights of Eldritch Yule. The climactic chamber, a convergence point of cosmic energies, revealed the true purpose of the Canticles. This cosmic prophecy bound the fate of myriad worlds to the eldritch celebration.

In a kaleidoscope of astral hues, the Eldritch Council unveiled the intricate patterns of destiny, each thread representing a life touched by cosmic events. Once shrouded in mystery, the Canticles now stood as a testament to the cosmic interplay between mortals and eldritch forces. This dance transcended time and space.

As the astral revelation reached its zenith, a cosmic resolution emerged. The Eldritch Council, custodians of the cosmic balance, guided the threads of destiny toward a harmonious conclusion. The eldritch energies, having left their indelible mark on the mortal realm, were now woven into the very fabric of the astral dominion.

The Climactic Chamber bathed in the astral glow of resolution, became a nexus of cosmic harmony. Once entangled in the cosmic tug-of-war, the interwoven fates found equilibrium under the Eldritch Council's watchful gaze. The Canticles, their purpose fulfilled, resonated with a final cosmic chord, marking the end of the 12 Nights of Eldritch Yule and the beginning of a new celestial cycle.

In the wake of the astral revelation, the Eldritch Council's Realm stood as a testament to the cosmic order restored. Once charged with the echoes of cosmic reckoning, the Climactic Chamber faded into astral serenity, leaving behind a sense of cosmic balance that transcended the boundaries of mortal understanding. The interconnected worlds, their destinies aligned, continued their journey through the astral tapestry, forever marked by the eldritch celebration that had unfolded across the realms.

In the aftermath of the astral revelation, Dr. Evelyn Blackthorn stood at the heart of the Eldritch Council's Realm. In this realm, cosmic forces governed the fate of interconnected worlds. The consequences of unlocking the Canticles weighed heavy on her shoulders, and the air in the astral dominion held a sense of cosmic resonance as she faced the enigmatic beings who presided over the celestial balance.

Once known as a mysterious guide, Professor Nathaniel Eldritch has now revealed himself as a cosmic mentor with a connection to the Eldritch Council. He is standing beside Dr. Blackthorn and assisting her in understanding the intricate patterns of destiny unveiled in the Climactic Chamber. With its otherworldly hues, the astral dominion is a canvas upon which the cosmic revelation paints a story of interconnected worlds and their shared destiny.

The Eldritch Council, ethereal and timeless, extended their astral presence toward Dr. Blackthorn. Their forms transcended mortal understanding, embodying the cosmic wisdom that governed the intertwined tales. The Eldritch Council acknowledged Dr. Blackthorn's role in the cosmic revelation with a gesture that echoed through the astral resonance.

In the silence of the astral dominion, Professor Eldritch spoke, unraveling the cosmic truths embedded in the Canticles of Yule. Once shrouded in mystery, the eldritch destiny now stood before Dr. Blackthorn like an astral tapestry woven with threads of interconnected worlds. The Eldritch Council, custodians of cosmic balance, guided her through the revelations, offering insights into the purpose that bound the fate of myriad worlds to the eldritch celebration.

As the cosmic resolution unfolded, the intertwined worlds found equilibrium under the watchful gaze of the Eldritch Council. Having served their purpose, the Canticles resonated with a final cosmic chord that echoed through the astral dominion. The Eldritch Council's enigmatic presence, timeless and unyielding, bestowed a cosmic blessing upon Dr. Blackthorn, acknowledging her role in the cosmic tapestry.

Now bathed in the serene glow of resolution, the astral dominion became a testament to the restored cosmic order. The Eldritch Council's Realm symbolized interconnected destinies and the harmonious conclusion the 12 Nights of Eldritch Yule brought forth. As Dr. Blackthorn, guided by Professor Eldritch, contemplated the astral serenity around her, she knew that the intertwined worlds would continue their journey through the celestial tapestry, forever marked by the eldritch celebration unfolding across realms.

The Eldritch Council's Realm stood as a cosmic seat of power. In this ethereal expanse, the fate of interconnected worlds was deliberated by enigmatic cosmic beings. The astral dominion, bathed in celestial hues, served as the stage for cosmic discussions that transcended mortal understanding. The Eldritch Council, timeless custodians of cosmic balance, gathered in the cosmic seat of power to oversee the harmonious resolution by the 12 Nights of Eldritch Yule.

The astral tapestry that adorned the cosmic chamber told the stories of myriad worlds, their destinies intricately woven into the fabric of the Eldritch Council's Realm. Each thread represented a realm touched by the cosmic revelation, and the enigmatic beings presiding over the cosmic seat of power held the key to maintaining the delicate balance that bound these realms together.

As Dr. Evelyn Blackthorn, accompanied by Professor Nathaniel Eldritch, stood in the presence of the Eldritch Council, the astral resonance of the cosmic seat of power echoed with the cosmic truths embedded in the Canticles of Yule. The beings, with forms that transcended mortal comprehension, extended their astral influence toward Dr. Blackthorn, acknowledging her pivotal role in the intricate dance of interconnected worlds.

The Eldritch Council's deliberations resonated through the astral dominion, their discussions shaping the destiny of realms entwined during the cosmic celebration. The cosmic seat of power became a nexus where the threads of fate converged, and the beings, guardians of the celestial balance, considered the implications of the eldritch revelation.

As the discussions unfolded in the cosmic seat of power, the astral tapestry shifted, reflecting the newfound equilibrium brought about by the intertwining tales. The Eldritch Council's Realm, radiant with cosmic wisdom, bore witness to the resolution of the cosmic entanglement, and the fate of interconnected worlds found its place in the harmonious order dictated by the Eldritch Council.

With its timeless presence and astral grandeur, the cosmic seat of power became a symbol of cosmic governance, ensuring that the interconnected destinies of the worlds would continue to unfold in harmony. Dr. Blackthorn, guided by Professor Eldritch, observed the cosmic tapestry within the Eldritch Council's Realm, knowing that the astral nexus held the key to the ongoing celestial journey of the realms touched by the 12 Nights of Eldritch Yule.

Dr. Evelyn Blackthorn stood resolute in the cosmic seat of power, facing the Eldritch Council with unwavering determination. The astral dominion pulsated with the weight of consequences as the enigmatic beings, guardians of cosmic balance, focused their otherworldly gaze upon her. The consequences of unlocking the Canticles of Yule and entwining the destinies of worlds manifested in the cosmic tapestry that adorned the astral chamber.

The Eldritch Council, beings of timeless wisdom, communicated through ethereal resonance, their voices echoing within the astral dominion. With a sense of humility, Dr. Blackthorn acknowledged the cosmic repercussions of her actions. The interconnected destinies of worlds, woven together by the eldritch revelation, now unfolded before her in a celestial panorama.

The Eldritch Council's forms transcending mortal understanding emanated a sense of cosmic understanding. Professor Nathaniel Eldritch stood by Dr. Blackthorn's side, his presence an anchor in the astral sea of consequences. The beings deliberated, their astral influence shaping the fate of the realms touched by the 12 Nights of Eldritch Yule.

As the discussions progressed, the implications of unlocking the Canticles became increasingly apparent. The destinies of once-separated worlds were now intricately interwoven, each contributing to a cosmic tapestry where the threads of fate danced in harmony.

Dr. Blackthorn, guided by her quest for knowledge and the desire to understand the Canticles, had become an unwitting catalyst for the cosmic dance. The Eldritch Council, with their timeless wisdom, acknowledged her role and the interconnected destinies that had emerged from the Eldritch celebration.

The astral dominion resonated with a sense of resolution as the Eldritch Council unveiled the consequences with cosmic clarity. Though facing the weight of her actions, Dr. Blackthorn sensed a cosmic harmony in the intertwining destinies. The beings, custodians of the celestial balance, conveyed a sense of approval, acknowledging the necessity of the cosmic revelation.

As the astral chamber reverberated with cosmic echoes, Dr. Blackthorn realized that the consequences of unlocking the Canticles were not solely burdensome; they carried the promise of a cosmic journey that transcended the boundaries of mortal understanding. Though profound, the destinies of interconnected worlds had found a new equilibrium, and the consequences held the potential for a harmonious cosmic tapestry.

As the cosmic tapestry unfolded in the astral dominion, the revelation of Professor Nathaniel Eldritch's true nature resonated through the chamber.

Once veiled in mystery, the enigmatic mentor was now revealed as a cosmic conduit, intricately connected to the Eldritch Council and the astral realm.

The Eldritch Council acknowledged Professor Eldritch with a cosmic nod, recognizing his integral role in guiding Dr. Evelyn Blackthorn through the labyrinth of cosmic revelations. His connection to the astral dominion ran deep, a testament to the cosmic knowledge that permeated his being.

Professor Eldritch, no longer confined to the shadows of ambiguity, stepped forward, his form bathed in astral luminescence. His eyes, reflecting the cosmic constellations, held a profound wisdom that transcended mortal understanding. The strands of his existence were interwoven with the celestial threads that governed the fate of interconnected worlds.

Professor Eldritch spoke of his purpose as a cosmic mentor with a resonant voice that echoed through the cosmic chamber. He revealed how he had been a guardian of the Canticles of Yule, guiding those who sought the cosmic revelations embedded within the eldritch prophecy.

The revelations continued, unraveling the story of Professor Eldritch's journey through the ages, witnessing the ebb and flow of cosmic events. His role as a conduit between mortal realms and the Eldritch Council became apparent, a bridge between the seekers of knowledge and the enigmatic beings who governed the astral dominion.

Absorbing the cosmic truths, Dr. Blackthorn felt profound gratitude and awe for her mentor. Once shrouded in uncertainty, the cosmic mentorship now stood as a testament to the intricate dance of destiny orchestrated by the Eldritch Council.

The astral dominion resonated with a harmonious cosmic melody as the revelations climaxed. Professor Eldritch, his form radiating with astral brilliance, stood beside Dr. Blackthorn, a cosmic guide in the celestial journey that unfolded through the 12 Nights of Eldritch Yule. The cosmic mentor and his protege, bound by the threads of fate, faced the astral dominion with a shared understanding of the intertwined destinies that transcended the boundaries of time and space.

Within the cosmic seat of power, the Eldritch Council convened their astral forms, resonating with otherworldly energy. Standing amid the enigmatic cosmic beings, Dr. Evelyn Blackthorn braced herself for the revelation of the true purpose of the Canticles of Yule.

The Eldritch Council's essence, intertwined with the very fabric of the astral dominion, began to weave a tale that transcended mortal comprehension. Embedded with cosmic knowledge, the Canticles harbored a prophecy that spanned the epochs, intertwining the destinies of worlds in a grand cosmic tapestry.

As the Eldritch Council spoke in harmonious unison, the astral dominion vibrated with the resonance of the cosmic prophecy. It foretold a celestial dance where the threads of fate from various realms converged and diverged in an intricate pattern of cosmic choreography.

The Canticles revealed to be more than a mere collection of verses, held the key to understanding the cosmic forces that governed the interconnected worlds. Each line, a celestial sigil, resonated with the energies shaping the destinies of those seeking wisdom.

The true purpose of the Canticles became clear—they were a guide. This cosmic roadmap illuminated the paths traversed by the seekers of knowledge. The Eldritch Council, as stewards of the astral dominion, safeguarded the delicate balance between mortal realms and the cosmic energies that permeated existence.

Dr. Blackthorn, her mind a vessel for the cosmic revelations, felt a profound connection to the celestial dance unveiled by the Eldritch Council. The cosmic prophecy spoke of cycles, beginnings, and endings, and cosmic energies converging and dispersing like the ebb and flow of celestial tides.

The Eldritch Council, their astral forms pulsating with the cosmic essence, bestowed upon Dr. Blackthorn the knowledge to decipher the celestial sigils within the Canticles. The cosmic mentorship of Professor Nathaniel Eldritch, now fully revealed, played a pivotal role in guiding her through the intricate layers of the prophecy.

As the cosmic revelation echoed through the astral dominion, Dr. Blackthorn embraced her role as a guardian of the Canticles, a seeker of cosmic truths. The true purpose of the eldritch verses became a beacon of cosmic wisdom, illuminating the interconnected destinies of worlds and the eternal dance of cosmic forces that unfolded through the 12 Nights of Eldritch Yule.

Within the climactic chamber of the Eldritch Council's Realm, the astral energies pulsed with a harmonious resonance, creating a cosmic symphony that transcended the boundaries of time and space. The interwoven realities of interconnected worlds converged at this focal point, where the threads of fate were intricately woven and delicately balanced.

Dr. Evelyn Blackthorn stood at the heart of this celestial nexus, surrounded by the cosmic entities and the ethereal glow of the astral dominion. The interplay of energies from diverse realms manifested as shimmering threads, each representing a different reality and the lives entangled within the cosmic tapestry.

As the Eldritch Council guided Dr. Blackthorn through the astral convergence, she witnessed glimpses of otherworldly landscapes, heard echoes of distant realms, and felt the temporal currents that flowed through the cosmic fabric. The interwoven realities revealed a delicate dance of cosmic forces, where destinies collided and harmonized in a cosmic ballet.

The astral threads, radiating with the hues of myriad realms, intertwined and embraced, forming a living tapestry that depicted the interconnectedness of existence. Time, a fluid essence within the climactic chamber, wove through the threads, creating a dynamic mosaic of past, present, and future.

Dr. Blackthorn, now attuned to the cosmic energies, sensed the weight of responsibility that came with unraveling the true purpose of the Canticles. The interwoven realities required a delicate touch, a cosmic awareness that transcended mortal understanding.

As the Eldritch Council presided over the astral convergence, the climactic chamber resonated with the cosmic echoes of interconnected worlds. The delicate balance within this cosmic tapestry held the key to preserving the harmony of existence. Dr. Blackthorn, guided by the revelations within the Canticles, stood as a guardian of the interwoven realities.

In the celestial dance of astral energies, the climactic chamber became a nexus where destinies collided, the interwoven threads of reality converged and diverged, and the true purpose of the Canticles unfolded. This cosmic revelation echoed through the astral dominion, leaving an indelible mark on the interconnected worlds.

Guided by the cosmic wisdom of the Eldritch Council, Dr. Evelyn Blackthorn and Professor Nathaniel Eldritch embarked on a journey within the astral dominion to restore the delicate balance that intertwined the cosmic threads of interconnected worlds. The luminous chamber resonated with the collective energies of diverse realms as the trio worked in unison to untangle the intricacies of the cosmic tapestry.

Each astral thread was examined meticulously, representing a world within the interconnected realities. The Eldritch Council, enigmatic cosmic beings with an understanding that transcended mortal comprehension, imparted their insights to Dr. Blackthorn and Professor Eldritch. Together, they navigated the complex intersections of destinies, striving to mend the temporal and spatial rifts that had been inadvertently woven into the fabric of existence.

As the trio delved into the astral convergence, they encountered pockets of imbalance where the cosmic energies had become entangled in unforeseen ways. Drawing upon his cosmic knowledge, Professor Eldritch unraveled the knots within the threads, allowing the Eldritch Council to weave a harmonious pattern that restored equilibrium to the interconnected worlds.

The astral dominion pulsed with a newfound resonance, signifying the restoration of balance. Once taut with discordant vibrations, the cosmic tapestry now swayed with a tranquil rhythm that echoed the unity of existence. The Eldritch Council, guardians of cosmic forces, observed the cosmic threads settling into a delicate harmony, ensuring that the destinies of interconnected worlds flowed seamlessly once more.

Dr. Blackthorn and Professor Eldritch felt the weight of responsibility lift in the astral chamber as the

Eldritch Council completed their cosmic work. The interwoven realities, now restored to balance, radiated with a luminous brilliance that transcended the boundaries of the astral dominion.

As the astral convergence concluded, the Eldritch Council acknowledged Dr. Blackthorn and Professor Eldritch, their cosmic guides in the journey to rectify the unintended consequences of unlocking the Canticles. The climactic chamber stood as a testament to the wisdom imparted, the cosmic revelation embraced, and the delicate balance maintained in the face of interconnected destinies.

With the restoration of balance, the astral dominion settled into a tranquil state, the echoes of cosmic resonance fading into a cosmic silence. The fate of interconnected worlds now rested in harmony, untangled and preserved within the cosmic tapestry that spanned the astral realms.

The restoration of balance within the astral dominion resonated across the interconnected worlds, leaving a tapestry of residual effects that echoed through time and space. As the harmonious energies settled, the threads of destiny began to shimmer with a renewed vitality, carrying the resonance of the cosmic nexus into the very fabric of existence.

In the wake of the astral convergence, subtle ripples traversed the timelines of the interconnected worlds. Temporal anomalies and echoes of cosmic forces manifested, leaving traces of the profound events that unfolded during the 12 Nights of Eldritch Yule. The residual effects, like whispers in the cosmic wind, whispered tales of unity, cosmic wisdom, and the delicate dance of interconnected destinies.

Throughout the realms, individuals who had unwittingly become part of the cosmic tapestry were touched by the lingering energies of the Eldritch

Council's intervention. Those who had navigated cosmic challenges during the Yuletide festivities now experienced a subtle awareness, a connection to the greater cosmic truths that bound their worlds together.

In some corners of existence, the residual effects manifested as glimpses into alternate timelines, where the interwoven destinies of the protagonists took unexpected turns. Familiar faces encountered unfamiliar circumstances, and the echoes of cosmic resonance played out in myriad ways, revealing the malleability of destiny within the interconnected realms.

Once visited through the stellar stockings, the celestial realms pulsed with a renewed vibrancy as the residual effects of cosmic intervention continued to weave their influence. Celestial beings observed the changes with an otherworldly curiosity, recognizing the intricate dance of fate guided by the cosmic revelations of the Eldritch Council.

As time unfolded, the interconnected worlds adapted to the residual effects uniquely. Relationships forged under the cosmic mistletoe, temporal anomalies unraveled by the candles, and celestial journeys through stellar stockings left indelible marks on the collective consciousness of the realms. The tapestry of existence, now infused with the cosmic wisdom of the Eldritch Council, bore witness to the enduring legacy of the 12 Nights of Eldritch Yule.

The astral dominion settled into a serene equilibrium, and the residual effects became a testament to the cosmic interplay that transcended the boundaries of individual worlds. The interconnected destinies, forever changed by the midnight reckoning, embraced the residual echoes of cosmic revelation, ensuring that the threads of existence continued to weave a story of unity, balance, and the enduring power of cosmic forces.

Having faced the cosmic reckoning and unraveled the profound mysteries within the climactic chamber of the astral dominion, Dr. Evelyn Blackthorn emerged as a guardian of cosmic balance. The weight of the Canticles of Yule, once a burden on her shoulders, transformed into a mantle of cosmic responsibility.

In the wake of the midnight reckoning, Dr. Blackthorn found herself attuned to the delicate vibrations of interconnected worlds. The residual effects of the Eldritch Council's intervention had woven her into the fabric of existence, granting her an otherworldly awareness of the cosmic forces at play.

Guided by the wisdom acquired during her journey, Dr. Blackthorn embraced her newfound role as a guardian. She became a vigilant observer of the cosmic threads, ensuring that the delicate balance restored by the Eldritch Council remained undisturbed.

Her connection to the Canticles of Yule granted her insights into the ebb and flow of the astral dominion, allowing her to navigate the complexities of the interwoven destinies.

As a guardian of cosmic balance, Dr. Blackthorn traveled between realms, her presence a stabilizing force in the face of potential cosmic disturbances. She walked the ethereal landscapes of the celestial realms, checked the mechanisms of Montgomery Clockworks, and lingered in the intimate warmth of the Montgomery Residence, ensuring that the residual effects of the 12 Nights of Eldritch Yule continued to harmonize with time.

Her encounters with individuals touched by the cosmic revelations became moments of guidance and reassurance. Whether it was Elizabeth navigating emotional turmoil, Thomas guarding the mistletoe's cosmic energies, or Sarah and Samuel returning from their celestial journey, Dr. Blackthorn's cosmic insights provided solace and understanding.

In the astral dominion's climactic chamber, where the Eldritch Council deliberated over the fate of interconnected worlds, Dr. Blackthorn stood as a representative of humanity—a guardian who had faced the consequences of unlocking the Canticles and emerged with an enlightened understanding of cosmic balance.

The echoes of her journey resonated through the interconnected realms, reminding all who had played a part in the cosmic tapestry that the delicate dance of destiny required guardians—those attuned to the cosmic forces that shaped the interwoven realities of existence. And so, Dr. Evelyn Blackthorn, the guardian of cosmic balance, continued her vigilant watch over the intertwined destinies, forever changed by the transformative journey through the 12 Nights of Eldritch Yule.

As the cosmic nexus embraced the final notes of the astral dominion's deliberation, a climactic resonance echoed through the Eldritch Council's Realm and the climactic chamber. The astral threads that had intricately woven the destinies of interconnected worlds pulsed with a harmonious rhythm. This cadence spoke of cosmic resolution and the echoes of intertwined destinies finding a delicate equilibrium.

In the Eldritch Council's Realm, the enigmatic cosmic beings witnessed the culmination of their guidance and the restoration of balance. Once a stage for the cosmic tug-of-war, the climactic chamber now stood as a testament to the collaborative efforts between cosmic entities and guardians of balance. With the wisdom gained from the Canticles of Yule, Dr.

Evelyn Blackthorn played a crucial role in harmonizing the cosmic forces that had teetered on the brink of chaos.

The resonance lingered in the air, a melody that whispered through the cosmic tapestry. The Eldritch Council, their forms ethereal and radiant, acknowledged the success of the cosmic reckoning. With its cosmic seat of power, the astral dominion became a tranquil haven where the fate of interconnected worlds found repose.

As the climactic chamber and the Eldritch Council's Realm gradually faded from view, a profound sense of cosmic resolution permeated the remaining echoes. The intertwined destinies, once entangled in the cosmic dance, now reverberated with a newfound harmony. The guardians of balance, Dr. Blackthorn among them, continued their vigilant watch over the delicate threads that connected realms, time, and existence.

As the last traces of the Eldritch Council's Realm dissipated, the cosmic nexus embraced a serene stillness. The climactic resonance marked not just the conclusion of a cosmic journey but the beginning of a new cosmic cycle—one where the echoes of intertwined destinies would resonate in the vast tapestry of the astral dominion, forever leaving a trace of the 12 Nights of Eldritch Yule.

Afterword

As the final echoes of the cosmic reckoning subsided, Magnum Tenebrosum, a silent observer of the unraveling mysteries of the Eldritch Yule, found solace in the aftermath. The cosmic tapestry, intricately woven through the twelve haunting nights, beckoned contemplation. In the hallowed halls of the Eldritch Council's Realm, where astral dominion governed the interconnected worlds, a reflection on the interplay between cosmic horror and the cherished traditions of Christmas took form.

The inspiration behind this anthology emerged from the depths of personal experiences, as shadows danced with memories and literary influences that whispered secrets of the unknown. Magnum Tenebrosum, the weaver of tales, revealed the unexpected—the fusion of eldritch terror and the warmth of Christmas themes. The dance was delicate, a cosmic waltz that unveiled unexpected harmony. It was a journey into the realms where the terror of eldritch entities heightened the glow of festive traditions in an enchanting juxtaposition.

Gratitude flowed for those who ventured alongside Magnum Tenebrosum through these twelve mystical nights. It was a shared exploration, a joint venture into the cosmic unease and festive enchantment that marked the tapestry. Characters, guided by cosmic patrons—The Eldritch Council—tangled destinies in a dance that surpassed the boundaries of fiction.

As the reader closes the pages, the lingering sense of cosmic unease remains—an indelible mark like faint echoes of eldritch forces disturbing the fabric of reality. Beyond the veil of the cosmic unknown, mysteries persist, inviting contemplation. The Eldritch

Council, enigmatic cosmic patrons, presided over destinies, leaving a subtle disturbance that will endure in the recesses of thoughts.

With the eternal nightfall descending, Magnum Tenebrosum leaves the reader with a poetic image—a metaphor encapsulating the essence of "12 Nights of Eldritch Yule." Picture the cosmic tapestry continuing to unfold, revealing the profound interplay between darkness and light, horror and warmth, in the eternal dance of the unknown—a dance that transcends time and space, weaving destinies in a tapestry that stretches beyond the boundaries of comprehension.

Magnum Tenebrosum